A PAW-SIBLE THEORY

(A Murfy the Cat Mystery)

by

Anna Kern

Copyright 2014 by Anna Kern

For information, email **Cozy Cat Press**, cozycatpress@aol.com or visit our website at: www.cozycatpress.com

COZY CAT
P R E S S

ISBN: 978-1-939816-54-2

Printed in the United States of America

Cover design by Katherine Janda
http://tea-and-jellybeans.tumblr.com

1 2 3 4 5 6 7 8 9 10

DEDICATION

To my son, James, who encouraged me from the start and patiently read the many versions of the first two chapters.

ACKNOWLEDGEMENTS

Thank you to my first readers for their insight and encouragement: Teresa Allan, Joann Gennari, and Lois Berardi Moltane. Thank you also to my publisher, Patricia Rockwell, for making it all possible.

"Thou art the Great Cat, the avenger of the Gods, the judge of words, the president of the sovereign chiefs and the governor of the holy Circle, thou are indeed...the Great Cat."—Inscription on the Royal Tombs at Thebes

"A cat is more intelligent than people believe, and can be taught any crime."—Mark Twain

CHAPTER ONE: *In a Cat's Eye*

In April of this year, a crime was committed in the historic district of Beachside, a tourist town, not beachside as the name implies, but about three miles inland on the east coast of Florida.

The neighborhood surrounding the old downtown business area, and still in the process of revitalization, is a mix of architectural styles as are the people who live there a mix of young couples with children, as well as middle-aged and older retired folks who have lived there many years.

According to the dictionary definition, my human fits in the middle-age category. As far as I'm concerned, she is whom she has always been: Alyx Hille, five feet three inches tall, brown hair cut in a short, shaggy sort of style, hazel eyes, and a beautiful smile. She shares her home with two quirky female felines and me.

My name is Murfy. I'm also a Felis catus, only different—even though I look and behave like an ordinary longhaired, cream tabby with green eyes. So far, Alyx is the only one who has reason to believe that I'm not—ordinary that is.

On Saturday April 16, casually dressed in tan, cropped pants and a coral top, Alyx listened to the animated weather forecaster on the local news promise the kind of day that brought frostbitten northerners down south at that time of year: clear blue sky, mild temperature, and low humidity. I don't know why, but she often apologized to visitors when the weather was less than perfect as if providing good weather was her personal responsibility. Strange as it seems, she wasn't alone in that, others did the same thing.

Alyx reached for the remote, and the promo for what was coming up next caught her attention.

"Incarcerated ten years for a crime he didn't commit, John Biggs was released from prison at noon yesterday. Listen to what his defense attorney David Hunter had to say."

"The ugly truth is that we don't live in a perfect world and for the sake of order, a judicial system is in place that finds, judges and punishes those who commit crimes against society, and because it is an imperfect world, sometimes the system fails. Those responsible for dispensing justice can and do make mistakes, at times allowing the guilty to walk away free and punishing the innocent at other times. This time the system worked and justice is served."

David Hunter, considered handsome by human standards, looked the part of a successful attorney. The gray highlights at his temples accentuated his good looks, as did the perfect fit of his expensive gray suit.

Alyx turned off the TV in the living room, her favorite room in the house after she painted the walls antique white and added colorful Oriental rugs over the original wood floor. The new patio door, flanked by two tall windows, provided much needed light and a great view of the backyard for all of us.

As she walked past, I did a full body stretch and followed her to the kitchen where there was always a chance for a treat. She poured herself a fresh cup of coffee and carried it to the 1940's enamel-top table and chairs unearthed in her parents' basement a few years earlier and the inspiration for the kitchen design. When asked, she said the table was a nostalgic reminder of her mother rolling out piecrusts for the frequent family gatherings that ended with her death, the saw marks on one of the chairs attesting to its previous role as a sawhorse for her father. The lemon-yellow walls reflected the sunlight streaming in from the bank of windows in the breakfast nook. Everyday dishes and cutlery sat on the counter along with the breakfast items—eggs, bacon and pancake mix.

Alyx unfolded the morning paper but didn't show any interest in reading it.

"What do you think, Murfy?" she asked. "Should I have considered the offer? Will Maggie understand why I reacted so strongly? How do you think Ethan will take my suggestions? Will he listen this time?"

I figured she was probably vocalizing the thoughts meandering across her mind and I went back to the living room, leaving her sipping her coffee, and gazing out the window.

The stalker creeping up behind her had only one thought in mind; the brutal attack was swift, plunging Alyx into an abyss of darkness.

"I simply can't resist a cat, particularly a purring one. They are the cleanest, cunningest, and most intelligent things I know, outside of the girl you love, of course."—Abroad with Mark Twain and Eugene Field, Fisher

CHAPTER TWO: *Something Wrong*

The loud thud-crash bounced me out of my favorite chair and on my feet. Temporarily disoriented and unsure of what I had heard or where it came from, I zigzagged across the living room, torn between diving for cover and investigating the noise. Instinct told me to run; something else told me otherwise, and in that moment of indecision, Misty frantically fleeing from whatever she thought was chasing her, streaked past me and disappeared.

I listened for voices or other sounds and heard none.

The house was eerily quiet.

Alyx's bedroom door was wide open. My step hesitant, all senses focused on the job at hand, I crossed the threshold and nervously swept the room—nothing there, nothing out of place. I peered in the attached bathroom, stretching my neck as far as I could without actually entering, and nothing there either.

Belly touching the floor, ears close to my head, I crept down the dark hall toward the front part of the house where the partially closed door to the guest bath gave me pause; something was on the floor in front of the vanity. I pushed the door open and pounced, but the thing did not fight back—it was just a bunched up rug, the dim light giving it a sinister appearance. A quick glance over my shoulder assured me no one saw me attack the rug, and I moved on to the second bedroom where the two large windows left nothing hidden.

At that point, Misty appeared at my side from wherever she'd been hiding, apparently no longer in fear for her life and meowed once. A vigorous slash of the tail and she obediently fell in line behind me, her head turning from side to side, ears swiveling as we made our way to the kitchen.

Misty had questions. I had no answers. Something was very wrong. In the kitchen, I saw Alyx slumped forward on the kitchen table, a dark fluid oozing from a gash on her head. I navigated the littered tile floor, gingerly sidestepping the broken pieces of an earthenware pot more than a quarter of an inch thick, the kind that a first year pottery student would create, and lay down across her bare feet. I didn't know what to do.

Misty tried to tell me it wasn't my fault, but she was wrong. My job was to look after my human and I had failed. I appreciated her support, I really did, but it didn't make me feel any less responsible. I should have heard someone or something and warned her, but I fell asleep, heard nothing, saw nothing. Now Alyx was hurt.

Misty didn't understand and I couldn't explain it any better than that. Actually, I wasn't so sure I understood the responsibility part myself. I only knew that's how it was. The one thing I was sure of was that Alyx needed help.

I didn't have to be an expert on human physiology to know she was hurt bad. I leaped on the table and touched her nose with mine, relieved that she was still breathing. Ethan would know what to do, except he didn't live here anymore. The situation seemed hopeless. I lumbered away, head low, shoulders slumped, and then I remembered the conversation I overheard the night before.

My spirit restored, Misty and I padded to the foyer where we had a view of the street, the driveway, and all the activities in the neighborhood through the sidelights Alyx left bare for that purpose. There we waited still as doorstops positioned on both sides of the door, the imperceptible jerky movement of the tip of my tail the only sign of distress. For once, Misty had nothing to say, and in the silence, I let my mind wonder.

Knowing that I wasn't about to repeat anything he said, I was Ethan's confidante when he lived at home, and I knew it had been difficult for him to tell his mother that he wanted to move out. Ethan had been very close to his father before the divorce and his father's neglect after the divorce broke his heart. His mother's complete love had made it hurt a little less, but as he got older and learned to accept his relationship with his father for what it was, he confessed that sometimes he wished she didn't love him quite as much, at times feeling smothered by the intensity of her devotion.

It had taken him several days to figure out how to say it so she wouldn't be hurt and when he finally told her he wanted to move out, she agreed it was time for him to go and helped him put together the things he needed to setup house. Truth was, Alyx knew just about as soon as he did that he wanted to move out, and she had made it easy for him on purpose, but not because she was glad that he was leaving as Ethan might have thought.

Since then, their relationship had moved to a different level, and for the most part, Alyx was a friend and advisor. Apparently, Ethan had unwisely ignored her advice lately, and that's what she said she wanted to discuss with him when she'd invited him for breakfast the night before.

"For a man to truly understand rejection, he must first be ignored by a cat."—Anonymous

CHAPTER THREE: *A Likely Suspect*

Time isn't something cats are generally aware of and I don't know exactly how long we waited before Ethan finally showed up. Just as he took his keys out to unlock the door, Alyx's best friend and business partner, Maggie Broeck, pulled in the driveway.

Ethan appeared surprised to see her, clenched the keys in a fist, and waited for her to get out of the car, wasting precious time. He didn't look happy, not necessarily because he didn't like her, more than likely because when she was around, she tended to side with Alyx, and he usually lost the argument. I know that because I'd comforted him many a time over the unfairness of it all.

I noticed that Maggie, elegantly dressed in beige slacks, a creamy white, silk blouse, and wearing her signature diamond studs, had recently added two more diamonds to her right ear.

Ethan greeted her with his usual grin, and a peck on the cheek, "Hey, Maggie, having breakfast with us?"

"Sure am. Your mother called me last night and asked me to join you. She said she wanted to clear things up, but didn't say exactly what. She sounded a little mysterious about the whole thing."

"Maybe it's about that misunderstanding you two had the other day," replied Ethan.

"Well, she'd better have a good reason for getting mad at me the way she did, and one breakfast isn't going to make up for it," Maggie said, not in a joking manner. "By the way, have you had a chance to speak to her about that matter we discussed?"

"I was going to do that today; I didn't know you were going to be here," he said as he inserted the key.

"You can still do that; I'll just leave before you do. I have some work to do anyway."

Although communicating with my kind was never a problem, humans used words, and I didn't have that ability. I only knew two ways to convey my ideas—body movement and meowing, a language developed by the cat to communicate with his human. I tried to express the urgency of the situation by yowling, a sound coming from deep down my throat.

Misty understood immediately and picked up the chorus. Apparently, Ethan didn't understand. He unlocked the door and squatted to pet me. Frustrated to no end, I tried body language, stiffened and took off, hoping Ethan would follow.

"Hey, what's the matter with you? Aren't you glad to see me?" Ethan asked with some unease reflected in his voice.

He called out a greeting to Alyx and when she didn't answer, he dropped his keys on the bench by the door and instinctively rushed to the kitchen followed by Maggie. When he saw Alyx slumped over the table, he immediately checked for a heartbeat and yelled at Maggie, who was standing right next to him, to call 911. With shaking hands, he grabbed a kitchen towel and applied it to her head wound.

The ambulance arrived shortly after, followed by the Beachside police. I kept my eyes on Ethan who looked helpless while the paramedics took care of Alyx. Detective Smarts introduced himself to Ethan, surreptitiously taking note of his expensive clothes and his new eight hundred dollar watch, but he wasn't so sly that I didn't notice what he was doing.

"I understand you'll want to follow the ambulance to the hospital, but we will need your fingerprints and a statement sometime today," the detective said.

Ethan nodded absently as the paramedics placed Alyx on a stretcher.

"I'll appreciate it if you'll stop by the Osprey Avenue Station at your earliest convenience."

In a hurry to follow the paramedics to the hospital, Ethan asked Maggie if she could stay and take care of things. The Detective introduced himself to Maggie. "Al Smarts," he said, not looking at her but in Ethan's direction.

Ethan searched his pockets for his keys, turned full circle, his eyes darting about until he spotted them where he had dropped them. Smarts openly observed his every move, ignoring Maggie, even though she was talking and gesturing excitedly.

"I'm Maggie Broeck and I just cannot believe what happened here. This is such a quiet neighborhood. Who could have done this to her?"

I sprinted to the front door, and Ethan, keys in hand, saw that his car was blocked and jogged to the ambulance before it peeled out. Out of the corner of my eye, I saw Pooky, my other housemate, quietly disappear into the lush landscaping surrounding the renovated bungalow.

Too distraught to call anyone's attention to Pooky's escape or to speculate as to why Smarts had scrutinized Ethan so thoroughly; I pushed it to the back of my mind to think about later.

"Dogs come when they're called. Cats take a message and get back to you."—Mary Bly

CHAPTER FOUR: *If Truth Be Told*

I returned to my listening post under the dining room table, and tried to remain as inconspicuous as possible. Under normal circumstances, both Misty and I would be hiding somewhere in the house far from the strangers, but this was different—our world had been turned upside down and sideways. I had no idea when I was going to see Alyx again, if ever.

Smarts was interviewing Maggie, and being very solicitous as if he were following a page from a manual on police interrogation.

"Are you okay? Can I get you some water?"

"I'm fine, but I would like to sit down." She gestured to one of the two upholstered chairs. She sat in one of the chairs, he in another. Her hands were shaking and she clasped them on her lap.

"Tell me what happened."

"Alyx called me last night and asked me to come over before I went to the store. She said it was important that she talk to me but wanted to do it in person. I was surprised to see Ethan when I arrived because I know he's not an early riser, especially on weekends. He dropped his keys on the bench in the foyer and called out a greeting to his mother.

He must have sensed something was wrong when Alyx didn't answer, and he rushed to the kitchen. I was right behind him when we found Alyx pitched forward on the table, unconscious.

After what seemed like minutes but was probably only seconds, he checked for a heartbeat and yelled at me, standing right next to him, to call 911. His hands shook as bad as mine do now; he grabbed a clean kitchen towel and applied it to her head. I called from the kitchen phone, and we waited for help to arrive."

"What's your relationship to the victim?"

"Alyx is my best friend and business partner. We own Antiques & Designs on Ocean Street."

"How long have you known each other?"

"We met about four years ago when we were both taking classes at Beachside Community College."

"Did you see or hear anything unusual when you arrived?"

"Other than the cats at the door meowing loudly and generally acting strange when we walked in, I didn't see anyone or hear anything different that would have caught my attention."

"Do you know of anyone she was having problems with, anyone who would want to hurt her?"

She shook her head. "Alyx is a very likeable person; I can't imagine anyone wanting to hurt her."

"What about her son, what kind of relationship do they have?"

"They have a very close relationship—loving and respectful."

"Did they have any disagreements?"

"Just the usual stuff parents and their children don't see eye-to-eye on. Nothing serious."

"Like what, for example?"

She hesitated. "Well, she was worried about his spending habits. At first, she thought that maybe he was spending money because he was depressed, but he kept spending even after he started taking medication.

Shortly after graduating from college, he found a good job as a graphic artist with a local publishing company and like many young people who finally find themselves with a lot of money to spend, he spent all he had and what he didn't have.

I told her not to worry about it since he does make good money. He's young; he's not thinking about the future like someone our age would."

"What was he depressed about?"

"His first and long-time girlfriend broke off with him and he had a hard time dealing with it. He's off meds now. He just took them for a short time."

Detective Smarts was going over his notes and in the lull, a uniformed police officer carrying a large, black, case, walked in and went straight to the kitchen. Maggie wanted to know who the officer was and what he was carrying.

"That's our Crime Scene Investigation Unit of one— Mel and his basic crime scene equipment. The routine is always the same; walk one path through the crime scene to identify items that relate to the crime, taking care not to disturb evidence. He'll photograph and videotape the crime scene and send the evidence to the Department of Law Enforcement Laboratories. As you can imagine, they're very busy but they have a new computer system, so I'm confident we'll get fast results."

"Will that yellow tape come down when he's finished?"

"Depends on what he finds. More than likely, it will be down tomorrow."

She looked at her watch. "I'd really like to get to the hospital. Will it be much longer before I can go?"

"We still need to take your fingerprints, but if you prefer, you can come to the station to do it."

"How much longer before you can do it here?"

"Maybe another half hour or so."

"Since Alyx has Ethan with her and isn't alone, I guess I'll wait and get it over with."

Detective Smarts put away his pen, indicating he was through with her, and started to head to the kitchen to confer with his partner who came towards him, the two stopping to confer in the dining room. I could hear them easily from my post under the big maple table.

"Boomer, I have a gut feeling about this one ... cut-and-dry. Did you notice the expensive clothes the son wearing, the watch on his wrist, the car he drives? See what you can get from the neighbors."

I couldn't help expressing my feelings with a low growl as Smarts continued on through the dining room. He heard me, stopped, and glared. Intimidated, Misty looked away but I boldly glared back at the detective, my tail vigorously lashing the air. What could he do? Arrest me? How dare he call it a cut-and-dry case; the evidence wasn't all in yet and he was ready to wrap it up! I didn't like the man and the feeling was obviously mutual.

"Most cats, when they are out want to be in and vice versa, and often simultaneously."—Louis J. Camuti

CHAPTER FIVE: *Unscheduled Hospital Visit*

Citrus County Hospital was only two miles from Alyx's house. I could have walked the distance, but decided it would be quicker if I got a ride. When the ambulance took Alyx away, I thought I might never see her again; I wanted to make sure she was all right. I didn't think it would be a problem as I'd hitched rides before. I figured Maggie was preoccupied with other things and wouldn't notice me slip out the door behind her, slide in the back seat when she opened the car door, and flatten myself to the floor.

The short ride was tolerable and I made my presence known when she turned off the engine, making her jump when I landed in the passenger seat.

"Oh, Murfy … as if I don't have enough to worry about. What am I supposed to do with you now?"

She sounded exhausted rather than mad, and shook her head in resignation when I responded with a short *mwa-mwa*. She looked around, emptied the large tote bag she used for her fabric samples and I cooperated—allowing her to stuff me in the bag. What else could I do? It was my idea, after all. I did complain when she found a large piece of fabric in the trunk and tucked it over my head. I thought that was completely unnecessary. How was I supposed to see what was going on?

I pawed some of the fabric off to the side to get my bearings. As we entered the hospital, I could see Ethan on the phone, pacing up and down the hall outside of the ER. When Maggie reached him, he said he'd called the family and let them know what had happened. Some uncertainty, some shyness crept into his voice when he said that he'd also called his father.

Maggie took him by the arm and walked him to two empty seats in the waiting area just around the corner. Speaking in clipped sentences, she filled him in on what had happened after he left.

I lifted my head slightly for a peek around the room; Ethan saw my ears and his eyes opened wide.

"That's not …"

"None other," she answered before he finished the sentence.

She rearranged the fabric over my head. Someone with coffee walked by and Maggie handed the tote bag to Ethan, issuing a warning before she went in search of the coffee machine.

"You better stay put or you're going home, Murfy."

Ethan, who knew me better, said, "Oh, yeah, that will keep him in line."

Three cups of coffee later, Maggie saw one of her store employees coming down the hall. She pointed the woman out to Ethan and rose to meet her at a distance. Curiosity got the best of me, my ears swiveled for the best reception, and I listened closely.

"Charvette, what are you doing here? Are you here to see someone?"

"I just came to see about Alyx."

"How did you know she was here?"

"I have a police scanner I sometimes listen to. I was listening this morning when I heard the 911 call go out. I knew it was Alyx's address. What happened? Is she okay?"

She got a short version of what happened. "We don't know how Alyx is. We're waiting to hear."

"Would you like me to stay and keep you company?"

"Listen, I appreciate the thought and I'm sure Alyx would also, but I don't think Ethan would feel comfortable with other people here. I'll come to the store later to talk to you and Bernice and make some plans for our schedules. By then, I'll know more about Alyx's condition."

A man in a white coat introduced himself to Ethan as the doctor on duty, and Ethan placed the tote on the floor. Maggie excused herself and Charvette, appearing to look for something in her purse, slowly walked away.

"I'm Dr. Casey, and I'm happy to report your mother's vital signs are stable, and she's out of danger from the head wound. We ran some diagnostic tests on her and neither the CAT scan nor the MRI shows any brain damage. We now have her hooked up to an EEG to report her brain activity and, at this point, the prognosis is good. She could regain full consciousness at any time or she may do it in stages with no permanent damage, and it goes without saying, the sooner the better."

Happy to hear she was going to be all right, I purred maybe a little too loudly and Maggie nudged the bag with her toe.

"Any questions?"

"I'm sorry, Doctor Casey," said Ethan, "I've heard the terms before but I'm not sure I really know what those tests are. Can you give us a little more detail?"

"Sure. We do a wide variety of testing to help determine if brain injury may have occurred. There are two types of neurological tests: those that examine the structure of the brain, and those that examine the function of the brain. The CAT scan and MRI look at the structure of the brain. The EEG, electroencephalogram, examines the function of the brain. The CAT scan is superior at detecting fresh blood in and around the brain, and we'll repeat that one again, just to be sure. Does that clarify it?"

"Yeah, thanks," said, Ethan." Can we see her now?"

"Yes, of course you can. Stay as long as you want and don't worry about leaving, we will certainly call you if there is any change."

Maggie and Ethan went into Alyx's room in the Intensive Care Unit and sat quietly side-by-side, alert to the beeps and blips of the monitors. Reassured that Alyx was going to be all right, I didn't see any reason to stay. Imprisoned in the tote bag as I was, I couldn't see anything anyway. Besides, I was hungry and needed to use the litter box. Next time, I'd go it alone, but for the present, a soft meow was enough of a reminder.

"Listen," said Maggie. "I have to get this cat out of here before we get thrown out and barred from returning. I know you have to go to the police station sometime today, so I think it will work out for both of us if I leave and take care of a few things, and when I get back, I'll give you a ride home to pick-up your car so you can go talk to Detective Smarts. How does that sound?"

"Alright, I guess."

I popped my head out of the bag, took a last look back before leaving the room, and saw Ethan pull up a chair next to the bed, take Alyx's hand, and start talking to her.

"There are many intelligent species in the universe. They are all owned by cats."—Anonymous

CHAPTER SIX: *Too Much Said*

Maggie put the phone on speaker while she refilled our empty food and water bowls.

"Ethan, it's almost seven o'clock, where are you?"

He said he was still at the police station but would be leaving shortly and asked if there was any change in Alyx's condition.

"No, Ethan; she was the same when I left her," Maggie answered in a matter-of-fact way. The conversation ended; she slipped the phone in her purse; and picked up the magazine she had brought along and left the room.

Finished with dinner, I padded to my favorite chair for a nap and found it occupied; Maggie was sitting in it, her head bowed almost as if praying, though she had never struck me as the religious type.

She lifted her head when I landed on the arm of the chair. "She has to wake up, Murfy. I can't handle it all. Ethan might be in trouble. Smarts asked too many questions about him, and I may have given him too much information." She shook her head as if trying to shake the thought out.

Tired from all the activity, I ambled to my favorite hiding spot under Alyx's bed and tried to sort out what happened as best I could. I woke up when I heard Ethan's voice, surprised that I had actually fallen asleep. Apparently, all that thinking had exhausted me, and I realized that I didn't have as much control over my natural make-up as I thought I did.

I scampered to the living room so as not to miss anything and in case I did, Misty was already there.

"What happened at the police station? Why did it take so long to give a statement and get fingerprinted?" Maggie asked Ethan.

"To begin with, I waited for over an hour for Detective Smarts to show up and when he finally did, we were constantly interrupted by some other cop or ringing phone." Ethan sat forward a little. "He said they interviewed the neighbors as to what they saw or heard. And they checked the house and pot fragments for finger prints."

Ethan hesitated a moment as if the thought had just occurred to him, and panic crept in his voice. "You know, they were asking me questions like I might have had something to do with it."

Maggie appeared to dismiss the idea. "That's absurd. You? Hurt your mother?"

"It's not that ridiculous; they interviewed me for two hours and kept asking me the same questions over and over. They took my fingerprints and Smarts commented on the fact that there was no evidence of a break-in; whoever it was got in with a key or someone let them in. Since I made the pot used to hit her, my fingerprints are all over it and the rest of the house. Add to that, nothing was taken, nothing was disturbed."

"How do you know it's one of your pots?"

"I recognized the fragments. You told me at the hospital that they fingerprinted you too. Did Smarts say why?"

"He said it was because we were the ones who found her, whatever that means."

Ethan walked to the window and looked out. A puzzled look wrinkled his brow when he turned to face Maggie.

"He asked me about my bout with depression. He wouldn't tell me how he knew, but I guessed it must have been you. The neighbors don't know. Why did you tell him?"

"It just came out. He asked if you and your mother did any fighting and one thing led to another. I'm sorry, Ethan. I shouldn't have said anything but even if I hadn't, they would have found out somehow."

"I thought medical records were confidential. I guess it doesn't matter now, but I don't think they would have. And if that wasn't bad enough, they checked my credit and found out I'm in over my head."

"I don't know anything about that. Does your mother know?"

He shrugged. "I think she might have an idea. That's what she wanted to talk to me about this morning."

He slowly paced back to his seat. "I don't get it. What do you think happened, Maggie? Do you have any idea who might have wanted to hurt Mom?"

"I don't know; your mom never even hinted at any problems with anyone, and I certainly never saw a problem with any of the people we know."

"What about that confrontation with Dan Ramsey at the Downtown Merchants Association meeting a couple of months ago?"

"Yes, there's that, but I really don't think he had murder on his mind. Did you mention it to Detective Smarts?"

"No, I forgot. Did you?"

She shook her head. "I forgot, too."

"That Detective Smarts kept referring to the fact that there was no evidence of a break-in, no evidence of a struggle. He asked me if I knew of anyone she might have given a key to the house."

She looked down at her shoes. When she didn't say anything, he continued, "I thought Mom gave you a key when she and Charvette went to that antique show in Georgia."

Still, no comment from Maggie.

"I guess you gave it back, so that just leaves me with a key to the house."

She looked away. "That's to be expected; you're her son, and you should have a key to the house."

I wondered why Maggie acted so strange when Ethan asked her about the key. It was no big deal if she didn't give the key back, so why?

When Ethan told Maggie he had decided it would be best if he stayed at the house so he could take care of us, and to make the hospital trips easier, she looked at him in alarm.

"Do you think that's a good idea? We don't know what happened here, Ethan. What if whoever did that to your mom comes back?" She reached for his hand. "Ethan, I don't feel right about you staying here."

He pulled his hand back and sank to the floor, flat on his back. I signaled Misty and we crept over closer to Ethan.

"Don't worry," he said; "I'll be okay. Besides, I have the cats to protect me." We meowed in agreement, bringing a smile to the humans' faces.

"See? They agree," he said.

Maggie didn't push it any further. "Okay, I can see you've made up your mind."

Ethan looked exhausted, as if the day's events had hit him all at once.

"This has been a very long day," Maggie said. "Why don't you go lie down while I make something to eat?"

Ethan didn't argue. Maggie waited for him to close the bedroom door, checked her phone, and walked out to the lanai to make a call. I slipped thru the door before she closed it and took cover next to the ornamental tree in the corner, not exactly hidden but not in full view either. Maggie conveniently sat at the bistro table next to the tree, and I edged closer so I could hear both sides of the conversation.

"Hi, George; it's Maggie. I'm just calling to thank you for the wonderful dinner last night. I had no idea you were such a good cook."

The name *George* didn't ring a bell at first, and then I remembered. George Lucas was Alyx's friend, the man who turned "trash into cash," so to speak.

"It was my pleasure, Maggie," I could hear his voice respond weakly through the phone. "I hope we can do it again, soon."

"I'd like that very much but something awful has happened and I'm afraid I may not have time to see you."

It sounded like an excuse but George didn't seem to take it that way.

"What happened, Maggie?"

Maggie told him the whole story. She concluded with, "I'm at Alyx's house now, and I convinced Ethan to take a nap. I swear, George, that boy has a stubborn streak in him that makes it hard to deal with him sometimes."

"What do you want him to do that he doesn't want to do?"

"He wants to stay at his mother's house and there's no changing his mind."

"As I'm sure you know, he was given responsibility at a young age. He thinks he knows best concerning himself."

"I know. Alyx told me that when she had to go back to work, the only job she could find was working as a clerk with the Police Department where they lived at the time. She had to be at work at seven in the morning. To be sure Ethan made it to school, and on time, she woke him up at six, made sure he was dressed, had breakfast and was ready to leave for school an hour after she left. Ethan never missed a day, unless he was sick, in which case, she had to depend on a kind neighbor to look in on him because she risked being fired if she took too much time off."

"At least he had breakfast," said George. "I read an article in *The Beachside Journal* that thousands of kids go to school without breakfast and just recently, the school board instituted a policy of free breakfasts for all students—the philosophy being that you can't learn on an empty stomach. It sounds like a good idea; only time will tell if it makes any difference."

"I don't have kids so I can't speak from experience, but it seems to me that experts are always looking for an explanation as to why kids don't do well in school. The educators blame the parents who in turn blame the teachers, and no one blames the student on whom rest the ultimate decision to learn."

"I didn't mean to change the subject, so all that aside, don't worry about Ethan; he was brought up well, and he really can take care of himself."

"I hope you're right, George. I don't want Alyx to get mad at me any more than she is already."

"What do you mean?"

I snuggled my head and ears a bit closer so I could hear the following conversation.

"Remember last night I told you that a real estate agent contacted me last week about selling our building?"

"Yes, you said Rupert approached you, with a tempting offer."

"Right. What I didn't tell you is that Alyx didn't want to hear it. I told her that our customers and clients would follow us no matter where the store was located. She wouldn't listen. I've never seen Alyx react that strongly to anything before, and I really didn't know what to make of it. More than that, my own reaction scared me—how angry I got at Alyx for not allowing me to explain that I didn't want to sell the building any more than she did, but that we should at least discuss it."

"I'm sure you'll get the chance to clear it up once she comes out of her coma."

"I hope it's soon, George. There's a ton of work left to do and we just accepted two new clients a few days ago."

"Is there anything I can help you with? I want to see more of you and I don't want to see you buried under with work."

"Thank you, George. You can help by taking me to breakfast tomorrow, but it has to be early."

"In that case, maybe I should come over and spend the night so we don't waste any time."

For some reason beyond my knowledge of humans, Maggie turned red.

"It doesn't have to be that early, George." She said that with a smile that lingered until she went back inside.

"There are two means of refuge from the misery of life – music and cats."—Albert Schweitzer

CHAPTER SEVEN: *A Sleepless Night*

Ethan's restlessness had kept me up all night. Still awake at three o'clock Sunday morning, I could barely keep my eyes open when Ethan rolled out of bed and powered on the computer.

I crept up behind him and perched on the back of the desk chair. The pictures on the screen looked like the machines I had seen in Alyx's room and I assumed he was looking up information that further explained what Dr. Casey had said about his mother's condition.

Ethan read aloud, "The wires attached to the scalp act like an antenna recording the brain's electrical activity at different frequencies, called alpha, beta, theta and delta activity."

That was all my brain could process, so I jumped off the chair onto the floor. I stopped listening, but Ethan continued reading. When he finally shut down the computer, I curled up with Misty who had been sleeping blissfully at the foot of the bed.

I didn't fall asleep right away as I thought I would. I couldn't stop thinking about the day's events. Foremost in my mind was who had tried to kill Alyx—and why?

I usually slept on Alyx's bed, so I was slightly disoriented when I opened my eyes and didn't see her there. Ethan was already up and, as was the routine when he lived at home, I jumped on the bathroom vanity for a drink of fresh water from the faucet before he stepped into the shower.

I missed Ethan when he moved out, but I would have missed Misty and Alyx just as much if he hadn't changed his mind about taking me along. Alyx had reluctantly agreed that he could take me with him when he moved out, but he a hard time finding a place that allowed pets. Actually, he told me in private that he'd found several places that allowed small pets; but he just couldn't bring himself to take me away from Alyx, let alone Misty—a small gray cat with blue eyes and a quirky personality.

Alyx had found Misty at a garage sale on one of her endless searches for unique items she planned to sell in the store later. I was elated when Alyx brought her home. I had often heard Ethan express his desire for a dog, and I was glad Alyx had always talked him out of it, telling him it wouldn't be good for the animal to be indoors alone all day since she and Ethan were both frequently out of the house. I figured I could have gotten along with a dog if I had to, but I definitely preferred the company of my own kind.

It was time for breakfast and I meandered to the food bowl in the kitchen where Misty was waiting for me. It seemed odd not to see Pooky sitting nearby. She always waited until everyone else had eaten before she approached the food bowl, her behavior that of a guest, careful not to overstep her bounds.

Misty and I had long been aware of Pooky's presence outside, waiting for Alyx to get the paper in the morning, and then again in the evening when she came home from the store. She was dirty and emaciated, her eyes—one green, and one gold—were glazed and unfocused, and what was left of her fur, matted, the few guard hairs around her neck sticking straight out. All in all, she looked pitiful. As Misty said, she looked like road-kill, and walked like a queen.

Pooky flourished under Alyx's care. Her black fur had grown long and glossy, her tail full and majestic and her eyes, still two different colors, once again bright.

The thing that bothered me most about Pooky was the fact that she liked to cuddle. I felt some pressure there because I just wasn't the type for all that mushy stuff and I thought she might make me look too aloof. Of course, my humans knew I cared for them. After all, didn't I share some of the stray lizards I caught on the screened porch with them? Didn't I, now and then, allow them the privilege of holding me for a minute or two? And didn't I reward them with uncensored purring? Still, I was fully cognizant of the fact that humans liked their cats to cuddle with them and Pooky had that role down pat.

There was no peace those first few months when Pooky came to live with us. Always called on to referee, I hated all that tail whipping, hissing, and spitting that went on with the two girls. They acted as if they were going to kill each other but never really did any damage; it was mostly noise and posturing. Unfortunately, things hadn't changed all that much, they still antagonized each other.

To my knowledge, no one had noticed that Pooky was missing, and obviously they weren't going to notice that morning either. They probably thought she was just hiding somewhere. Cats did that—hid in places humans never suspected, and then reappeared out of nowhere, their hideaway remaining a secret. The craziest and most dangerous place that I can think of where one of us hid was when Misty decided to take a nap in the washing machine.

I didn't see her jump in when Alyx left the laundry room to answer the phone, but I was there when she returned to finish loading the washer. Misty flew out and stomped away, clearly perturbed at being disturbed from her nap.

Dressed in the change of clothes his mother had suggested he leave in the closet just in case, Ethan was looking at the collection of his pottery displayed on the upper kitchen cabinets, near the ceiling. I thought that he was probably trying to figure out where the one that had been used as a weapon might have been.

I followed him back to the living room and out to the screened porch some called a lanai, which had originally been just a covered porch. Here was another of his larger pots, this time used in a corner display with plants and antique water cans—one of which, complete with paint spatters that Alyx had found in her parents' garage and was at least one hundred years old.

"How do you figure it, Murfy? Where did Mom have that pot? It could have been anywhere in the house; you know how she likes to move things around. Someone could have just grabbed the pot and waited for the right time to hit her with it."

Since nothing much ever escapes a cat's notice, I had a pretty good idea about the pot's most recent location, no matter how many times it might have been moved. Nevertheless, I made a mental note to ask the other felines about it.

I padded back to the kitchen; Ethan followed and, thinking aloud, he came to the same conclusion I had, that someone could have come into the kitchen from three different areas—guestroom, hallway, or dining room.

"If they came in from the guestroom or the hallway, Mom would have seen them, which means they must have come up behind her from the dining room, the question being, how did they get in without Mom hearing them, and with all the doors locked—that is, if they were locked? And why would someone want to hurt her?"

Those were all good questions that I hoped Detective Smarts was investigating.

"Cats are intended to teach us that not everything in nature has a function."—Garrison Keillor

CHAPTER EIGHT: *A Chilling Implication*

I looked out and saw that Ethan hadn't left yet. His car was still in the driveway and he was sitting in it writing on a notepad. Mrs. Leary, the next-door neighbor, was trying to get his attention as she slowly shuffled her way towards the car, all the while her dog, Smooch, was pulling on his leash in another direction.

Mrs. Leary, who had trouble outlining her lips with the red lipstick she always wore, was a genuine Florida native, and since she had lived and taught school here for most of her eighty years, she was a fountain of information about the area and its politics. She knew everyone and could tell you anything you wanted to know about what went on at City Hall, and often did.

"Hi, handsome; I'm glad I caught you. How is your mom?" she said loud enough to be heard across the street.

She didn't wait for his answer but went on to tell him that all the neighbors were talking about what happened, the older neighbors concerned that someone had targeted the neighborhood for robbery and that they might be next. He gave her a brief update on his mother and told her that since the police didn't know if this had been an attempted robbery or something else, they would be keeping an eye on the neighborhood for a while.

"I had Eddie Smarts in my class two years in a row in high school, you know. Who'd ever have thought he would one day be a detective?"

"Why is that a surprise?"

She laughed. "He was the class clown, always in trouble about some silly thing or other egged on by his best friend, our new Commissioner, Jack Shultz."

I found it hard to believe that Detective Smarts even knew how to smile. I certainly hadn't seen any evidence of it and the man's behavior toward me bordered on rudeness.

"As a matter of fact," she continued, "this is Smart's first case since his promotion after twenty years of service with the department." She moved closer and lowered her voice a notch. "I hear there's talk among the ranks that his promotion had more to do with his friendship with the Commissioner than it did with his investigative skills."

"Well, I sure hope he's done clowning around and gets busy catching the one who put Mom in the hospital."

Before Ethan could politely leave, they chatted for a few more minutes about some other kids she'd taught who now held important positions, including Everett Bixby, the District Attorney.

"I imagine Smarts is under pressure to prove himself and eager to put an end to the talk. I feel sorry for the poor soul he sets his sights on."

The implication was chilling.

"Women and cats will do as they please, and men and dogs should relax and get used to the idea."—Unknown

CHAPTER NINE: *A Mumbled Apology*

The Westminster chime of the doorbell woke me up from a sound sleep. Ethan's father, Bob, was standing there puffing on a cigarette. He rang the bell a second time and started to walk away, got as far as his car and turned back. He lit another cigarette with the one he'd finished and flicked the stub in the direction of the driveway, spotted the newspaper tossed in the yard that morning and sat down to read it. He scanned the front page, turned to the back page and a worried expression flitted across his face. He dialed a number on his cell phone.

"Helen, it's me. I'm going to be home a little later than I thought. Ethan isn't back and I'm going to wait for him."

Of course, I didn't hear what the other party said.

"Yes, honey, I know I said I would go with you, but this is more serious than his message said. We'll do it another time, okay?"

Smoke billowed around his head. "Are you still planning on pot roast for dinner? Can we have cherry pie a la mode for dessert?" He took a long drag, filling his lungs and exhaled.

"Fine, don't stress. I'll stop at the grocery store for the pie."

Bob had remarried shortly after he divorced Alyx, and with good reason Ethan didn't like his new wife. He told his mother that she always complained to his father about the mess he made while visiting, and she did it in front of him, usually leading to an argument and Ethan going home early. Eventually, the father-son relationship turned into one of distant relatives; an occasional phone call, with dinner three or four times a year.

Bob stood and took a step forward when he saw his son turn into the driveway. Ethan looked straight ahead, oblivious to everything around him as he followed the brick walkway to the front door.

Ethan, tall and handsome, had the same deep blue eyes and black hair as his father; his father's hair peppered with gray.

"Hi, Dad, what are you doing here?"

They shook hands, patting each other on the back in something resembling a hug.

"Looking for you, son. I stopped by your apartment and when I didn't find you there, I thought I might find you here before I checked at the hospital."

"Have you been waiting long?"

"Traffic is bad. I got here about fifteen minutes ago. The official Beachside Visitor Information website boasts that approximately four million visitors a year enjoy the beach and I think half of those four million visitors decided to visit this week."

The city hosted several special events during the year that brought as many as three hundred thousand visitors, per event, to the area. Fueled by the local newspaper editorials and local radio station's talk show hosts, these events were a source of on-going contention between the business community and the residents.

According to Alyx, the residents felt they were the losers in the struggle. The crowds attending the big name concerts on the beach made it almost impossible to get around town, diverting law enforcement from residential areas and often delaying emergency service. On top of that, the city levied higher taxes to cover the cost of the events while the local businesses, including those in surrounding cities and itinerant businesses, enjoyed the profits.

Spring Break was in full swing and the subject of daily articles in the newspaper concerning safety and the destruction of property wherever the college students stayed. Unfortunately, the safety issue came up more often than it should have—referring to several deaths that had occurred when drunken students tried to make their way from one balcony to another.

"Yeah, right? I was stuck in the traffic congestion the new bridge was supposed to eliminate and it took me more than thirty minutes to get across."

There was an awkward moment of silence before Ethan picked up the conversation again.

"Haven't heard from you in a while, Dad."

"I'm sorry, but I lost you cell phone number when I changed phones." The last part said with some embarrassment.

"Yeah, I see how that can happen, especially when you don't call the number much."

"You know how it is, son, time just seems to slip by."

Ethan had every right to feel as he did, but confronting his father on an emotional level was not his style and I wasn't surprised he dropped the subject.

"Yeah, Dad, I know how it is," he said, looking off into the distance, his chin jutting out ever so slightly.

He unlocked the door and invited his father in.

To my knowledge, Bob had never been inside before and he looked around appreciatively.

"Very nice. Your mother always had a knack for decorating. I'm glad she's finally doing what she apparently loves."

They sat across from each other, Ethan in my favorite chair, while Bob chose the tan, camelback couch. I settled on the coffee table and Misty picked the floor.

"Son, I'm sorry about your mom. The article in the *Beachside Record* doesn't say much more than what your message said."

He turned to the back page and read the short article in *The Police Scan* column.

"Saturday. Early this morning, Citrus County Hospital admitted local merchant Alyx Hille, part owner of Antiques & Designs. Her son, Ethan Hille, and business partner, Maggie Brock, found her unconscious and bleeding from head trauma.

Beachside police are investigating the incident. At this time, the police have no suspect or a motive for the attack. If you have any information, please call Detective Smarts at the Beachside Police Department."

"There's really not much more to tell," said Ethan, then filled him in on the few details not mentioned.

"Dad, I know you and Mom don't talk much, if at all, but do you have any idea who'd want to hurt her?"

Bob started to say something then hesitated, shrugged his shoulders, and rubbed the palms of his hands on his knees. "Well, son, when you're in business like your mom is, there's always the chance that you've made some enemies somewhere along the line. Envy and greed are always a good motive for murder, and statistics show that it's usually someone close to the victim who committed the crime."

Ethan looked puzzled. "What do you mean, Dad? You're not suggesting that I had anything to do with it, are you?"

"Of course I'm not suggesting you had anything to do with it. I'm merely answering your question."

"You think Maggie did it?"

"I didn't say that."

Silence followed.

"We haven't talked in a while, son. How are things going with you?"

"How do you think they're going? I'm worried about Mom."

"I meant with you personally before this happened."

"I guess, okay. Same as everyone else, not everything is perfect but I'm dealing with it."

Silence.

I had to give Bob credit for effort in trying to act like a father, thinking how hard it must be for him, not having had much practice at it.

"I know you're worried about your mother, and I know there's no sense in telling you not to worry, so I won't, but she's in good hands and I believe she'll wake up sooner than anyone expects."

Ethan nodded without comment.

"Okay. I'd better get going. I was wondering if you want to have dinner with Helen and me. She's making one of your favorites—pot roast, and cherry pie a la mode for dessert."

"No, thanks for the offer, but I've already made plans with Maggie. As a matter of fact, she should be here any time."

"All right, son. Call me if you need anything. I mean it."

"Sure, Dad, thanks for coming."

They shook hands at the door. Bob started to say something, and hesitated. I may have heard a note of regret in his mumbled, "I'm sorry about ... about everything."

When he left, Misty wanted to know why humans made their relationships so complicated. It was obvious they loved each other. Why couldn't they be more like cats and just be upfront about how they felt?

"My cat speaks sign language with her tail."—Robert A. Stern

CHAPTER TEN: *Coming Soon*

After his father left, Ethan trudged to his old room and fell forward on the bed. His cell phone jingled and he turned on his back. I crouched next to his head.

"Hey, Maggie what's up?"

"I'm on my way back from seeing a client and I'm calling to see how your day went and what you want for dinner."

"My day has been … full."

"You sound a little down. What happened?"

"I'll tell you when you get here."

"I won't get there for a while; tell me now."

"Okay, fine as long as you leave me alone after I tell you."

"I didn't sleep much last night and needed coffee when I got up this morning. I didn't feel like making it so I stopped at the café next door to Antiques & Designs. Novie came out with a tray of muffins and told me to take one for later. She asked about Mom, wanted to know what happened, and said she's going to send her flowers."

He switched the phone to the other ear, and I switched sides.

"Maggie, I'm so tired of people asking me what happened. I don't know what happened."

"You didn't say that to her, did you?"

He sighed in exasperation. "No, I didn't." He took a deep calming breath. "Then, when I turned left at the old Dixie Department Store building on the corner, I saw a large sign in the window with a picture of our building and *Coming Soon—Luxury Condominiums—* printed across it … but you know that already."

"You sound upset. Did the sign bother you?"

"It bothered me because it would really upset Mom if she saw it."

Maggie then asked him what he did at the hospital without commenting on what he had said. He took a deep breath and started to calm down. He told her he sat with his mother, occasionally talking to her, sometimes playing games on his phone or on the internet sending and checking e-mails.

"I left for a while when Marylyn Sims came to sit with her."

"Good; I'm glad Marylyn made it. She didn't think she would when she called me last night—something to do with her daughter needing a ride somewhere. Did you go home when you left?"

"Yeah, I went home to pack a few things and run some errands. Some other stuff happened but I'll tell you about it later."

I had been to Ethan's apartment before and could imagine Ethan running up the outside stairs of the two-story wood structure that was built to look like a seaside resort.

He had decorated the comfortable apartment himself. Alyx had offered to help. He declined, saying her style wasn't his style. This meant that he didn't want to end up with half the stuff she had in her store that she didn't have room to move. In the end, he asked for her input on furniture placement. He actually liked the suggestions she made and everybody was happy.

Ethan didn't answer the ringing phone in the kitchen and let the answering machine take the message from his aunt, Alyx's sister. I brought him toys to play with, Misty brought him her string, and we kept him busy until Maggie arrived with bags of take-out food from the local BBQ restaurant—ribs, chicken, baked beans, coleslaw, and rolls.

"One of the most striking differences between a cat and a lie is that a cat only has nine lives."—Mark Twain

CHAPTER ELEVEN: *An Unexpected Call*

Ethan carried the bags of food out to the table in the screened porch. Maggie started to unpack and he commented on the quantity.

"You can feed ten hungry people with all this. Are you sure you have enough?"

"You can handle it," she smiled.

As it turned out, none of the humans was very hungry, and there was plenty of food left over, although neither of them offered any of the leftovers to me or Misty. Ethan helped Maggie clean up, tossing the plates in the bags the food came in, and casually telling her about his father's visit.

"Dad stopped by. He left about a half-hour before you got here," he said, giving her a sidelong glance.

"Oh, and what did he have to say?"

"Not much. He got my message and just wanted to know what happened."

"That's it?"

"Yeah, and he asked me to have dinner with him but I told him that I had plans with you."

"I bet that went over big."

"Hey, I know you don't like Dad, but he didn't say anything at all about you," he lied.

Maggie retracted her claws. "I'm glad he came to see you," she said, giving him a hug.

Ethan reached for a can of soda, pulled the tab, and offered it to Maggie. She declined and he took a long swallow as they settled in on the patio chairs. Misty and I settled in too.

Maggie moved the conversation to another subject, asking Ethan about his job, whether he had requested any time off. He said he had spoken to his boss and there would be no problem taking off whenever he needed to.

"I got a message from Lea today."

"Are you surprised she called?"

"Well, yeah. The last time I spoke to her, she told me that she never wanted to see or hear from me again as long as she lived."

"Did she say why she called?"

"She said she heard about Mom and called to see how she was." He stretched out in the porch recliner.

"Don't try to read too much into it, honey. Lea is a sweet girl and that's just what I would expect from her."

"You don't think I should call her back, then?"

"I didn't say that. Just don't push ahead too fast, okay? She may have called simply to ask about your mom."

"Do you know what happened between us? Did Mom tell you?" he asked, sitting up sharply.

"Not really. I just know you broke off with her and she wasn't interested when you tried to get back with her. What I don't understand is why you ended the relationship in the first place."

"When we started going together, she was funny and adventurous, willing to try anything, but as time went by, she got serious about everything and wasn't fun to be around anymore. I thought it was because she didn't care about me anymore.

I knew I'd made a mistake the moment I told her I wanted to break it off, and I tried to get back with her about a week later," Ethan continued. "I think her pride was hurt more than anything else was, and she wanted nothing to do with me. The last time I tried to see her, she wasn't home; her roommate let me in, anyway. She told me Lea was seeing someone else, and sure, I could leave a note on her dresser. When I did, I saw another note that said, *"Thanks for not waking me. See you tonight. Steve."*

Steve was the guy we often met up with when we went out. She told me he was a longtime friend. Guess he was more than that. I don't know what hurt more, the fact I loved her and lost her or the fact that she lied about Steve. Either way, I don't know if I can talk to her without all that hurt coming back."

"I know what you mean, Ethan; I've had some experience with that myself." Maggie smiled and shrugged her shoulders.

If she was going to say any more about it, she didn't get the chance. Someone was pounding on the door.

"Thousands of years ago, cats were worshipped as gods. Cats have never forgotten this."—Anonymous

CHAPTER TWELVE: *Decision Time*

I ran ahead to see who was pounding on the door, and what was so urgent. I knew Ethan was in trouble as soon as he opened the door, and I saw Detective Smarts and his partner standing there with stern expressions on their faces. Maggie hurried to the door when Smarts asked Ethan to step off the porch. Ethan did as instructed and so did I.

"What's this all about? Do you have a suspect?"

"We're here to arrest you for the attempted murder of your mother, Alyx Hille."

Ethan laughed defiantly. Maggie's hand flew to her mouth in a gesture of disbelief.

Detective Albright read Ethan his rights. The laughing stopped once he was hand cuffed, his face devoid of any emotion, his eyes empty of feeling. I brushed against his legs offering him unconditional love and support. Ears back, tail bushed, doing my best to look as fierce as possible, I stalked over to Detective Smarts and snarled.

"Ms. Broeck, that cat is a menace and he's not on a leash. Please take him inside or I'll have to call Animal Control."

Maggie didn't comply right away; she placed a comforting hand on Ethan's arm before Detective Smarts led him to the squad car.

"Don't worry, Ethan; I'll call a lawyer and get you out as soon as possible, and I'll take care of things around here and with Alyx until you get back," Maggie said.

"Thanks, Maggie," was all he said.

As soon as the police had driven away with Ethan, Maggie sat heavily on the bench in the foyer, and I found a spot next to her. She buried her face in my abundant fur. I didn't mind; she needed a hug.

"You're lucky you're a cat and don't understand what's going on," she whispered. "Alyx in a coma, now Ethan arrested for attempted murder; what am I going to do?"

She stood abruptly. "I know one thing I'm going to do. Alyx isn't going to like it when she finds out, but it's for the best. His father has had a free ride for too long, if you ask me. It's time for Bob Hille to get involved in his son's life, whether he likes it or not."

I also made a decision. I'm no detective, but my human family was in trouble and I was the only one who could get to the truth. Based on a hunch, I decided to conduct my own investigation. I knew there was no way Ethan had anything to do with hurting Alyx, and I was going to prove it.

The fact that Pooky had run away bothered me. I couldn't think of any reason why she would do that—unless she saw something that might have panicked her. *Maybe,* I thought, *Misty saw or heard something I missed.* But first, I needed a snack; the shredded chicken Maggie had left on two paper plates in the dining room would do just fine.

When we were alone, Misty bombarded me with questions, some of which I couldn't answer such as why they took Ethan away, where did they take him, and when was he coming back. I didn't want to scare her, but I was just as bewildered by the events as she was.

As a rule, cats don't talk but have always been able to communicate with each other, and rumor has it that some uncommon cats have the ability to communicate the same way with humans. I told Misty I had something important to discuss with her and guided her to the dining room. I jumped up on the maple dining room table surrounded by four birdcage-back chairs all refinished by Alyx. I circled the centerpiece, a large white pitcher filled with wilted, yellow roses from the yard. I accepted that what had happened was beyond my control, and explained that if Ethan went to prison it wouldn't only ruin his life, it could damage Alyx to a point from which she might never recover. We had to help Ethan. Misty didn't see what we, being just cats, could possibly do to help since we weren't' even allowed to go outside.

I thought I had been patient enough with her. I jumped off the table with fur flying; landing softly on all fours, nose to nose. There was history to prove that the Egyptians once worshipped cats as gods. True, as Misty said, that was thirty-five hundred years ago in Egypt, give or take a few hundred years, and cats didn't have that kind of power any more but as individuals, cats still had humans in their service. Misty argued the point using Pooky as an example, how her humans abandoned her in the woods, miles from home.

Contrary to popular wisdom, a cat's brain is structurally similar to the human brain, and I could process vital information as quickly as any animal, the only difference being that what I considered vital was not necessarily what a human would consider vital. So sometime later, safe under Alyx's bed, I did some thinking.

From the beginning, the other two felines looked to me to explain things that they didn't understand and generally went along with what I said, not only because

I was bigger and stronger—my sixteen-pound size did help—but because I seemed to have greater knowledge of the laws, rules, and regulations that governed humans.

My decision to prove Ethan innocent didn't surprise me when I thought about what my mother had told me when she learned that I was adopting Alyx and leaving soon. There wasn't much she could tell me about my father. All she knew about him was that he came from a long line of great tabbies and that made me a pedigreed cat. The *M* on my forehead was proof of it. Unfortunately, not having the mark herself, she didn't know exactly what it meant. My feeling was that it was just a legend, but then again, who knows?

I fell asleep with that last thought in mind and woke up hours later to Misty's wet licks on my face, the earlier disagreement forgotten. I crawled out from under the bed on my belly, stretched front to back, sat back and washed my face. Misty helped by grooming my left ear. I sauntered to the food bowl with Misty trotting at my side. I wasn't happy to see an almost empty bowl but I didn't worry. Maggie had told Ethan she would take care of us, and I was sure she would, mostly because that's what Alyx would want her to do, but also because she was getting to know our personalities and I sensed she was starting to like us.

On Monday morning, the lawn service people were busy at their work, making the usual racket associated with lawnmowers, trimmers, and leaf blowers. The commotion outside kept Misty and me on the alert inside as we ran from one side of the house to the other side.

I wasn't expecting Maggie so early and didn't hear her car pull up, so I was somewhat unnerved when I heard the key slide in the lock. Maggie had lied; she had let Ethan assume that she didn't have a key when she did. I wasn't so sure I should trust her anymore and I deliberately took my time responding when she called.

The expression on Maggie's face was one of guilt when Misty and I showed up without Pooky, and she finally realized that Pooky was missing.

She began a search of the house; Misty following her around, helping her look in and under things. By the time she finished searching the house, the lawn service people had left. Maggie refilled the food and water bowls and went outside, a bag of cat treats in her hand. I hoped Pooky had not been terrorized out of the yard, if she still happened to be there, when the noisemakers arrived earlier in the day.

Mrs. Leary was sitting on her porch waving to Maggie, "Hold on a minute, dear, I want to talk to you," shouted Mrs. Leary walking across the lawn towards her.

"It's a shame about Ethan," she said. "I do hope he didn't have anything to do with what happened to his mother. Of course, no one in the neighborhood believes he did."

"Well, let's hope the jury believes it too or he's looking at possibly spending the rest of his life in jail."

"What about Alyx, how is she?"

"She's the same. Her doctor is still hopeful she'll wake up soon."

"I hope you'll let me know when she does; I'd like to send her a card."

"That's very thoughtful of you. I'll be here every day and have a lot going on. I'll try to remember to tell you, but feel free to ask me when you see me."

Maggie walked around the house once and went back to ask Mrs. Leary if she had seen Pooky—a longhaired, domestic black cat with different color eyes.

"Isn't that the stray that was going door to door begging for food a while back? The one that charmed Alyx into taking her in?"

"Yes, that's the one. Have you seen her?"

Mrs. Leary said she hadn't seen that particular cat in the yard but would be glad to keep an eye out for her.

I had given a lot of thought to Pooky's disappearance. I didn't know exactly why she ran away but I was convinced she knew something important. I thought I had caught a glimpse of her the previous day, and in the early hours of the morning, I formulated a plan. However, I needed Maggie's help to carry it out, and since I couldn't directly communicate what I wanted her to do, I had to rely on my knowledge of human behavior.

I wasn't surprised when Maggie came back inside with the treats but no Pooky. Something had made Pooky leave the safety of home and she wasn't going to be enticed by a few treats. I sniffed the treat Maggie offered from the bag in her hand, savored it in my mouth, and thought it was disgusting. Misty agreed and tried to bury it.

"I take it you don't like it," Maggie said, amused. "Let's see what else we can find."

She threw the treats in the trash and looked in the pantry for something else; my loud purring guiding her to pick just what we wanted.

Snack time over, Misty and I complied with Maggie's wish to play by chasing after the paper wads she tossed at us. Misty dragged her string over to play tug-of-war, and I joined in the game, pulling at the string, occasionally swatting at Misty until she decided she didn't want to share anymore and took it away.

Misty was obsessed with a thick, long shoelace from one of Ethan's athletic shoes. He had given her the shoelace after unsuccessfully trying to keep her away from his shoes. She would not let it out of her sight; if she wasn't laying on it, she was dragging it with her. She loved to play tug-of war. Sometimes she tossed it in the air, pouncing on it when it came down. When it fell on her, draping itself around her neck, she went about her business of keeping track of everyone, perfectly happy with it that way.

When she was really bored, she pretended she wasn't the one flicking the tip of her tail and would try to catch the rascal, rolling head over tail all over the floor, and I usually ended up playing a game of hide-and-seek with her—I hid and then attacked her as she walked by.

I chased after her with no intention of catching her. A few minutes later, she was back, her second favorite toy in her mouth—a sock tied in a knot.

She dropped the sock at Maggie's feet and waited for her to toss it, readying herself to retrieve it, low to the ground, her rear wiggling. She did this a few times then she sauntered over to her string and fell on it, protecting it from any predator.

Finally, tired of the games and anxious to begin the investigation, I decided it was time for Maggie to leave. I signaled Misty, and by previous arrangement, she ran in one direction, I in another.

Relying only on my knowledge of human behavior, unseen behind a large potted plant, I watched Maggie tidy up the living room and as she made her way to the front door, she picked up and tossed the toys in a basket by the couch. She was almost out the door, when she turned back and did just what I had been desperately willing her to do—she put food and water out on the screened porch and used a small empty pot to prop open the outside screen door a few inches.

Now I had another decision to make. Should I tell Misty? I concluded it would be better if she knew; less chance of her getting frightened and unwittingly messing things up, I reasoned.

"A cat has nine lives. For three he plays, for three he strays, and for the last three he stays."—English Proverb

CHAPTER THIRTEEN: *Witness Interviews*

As soon as Maggie locked the door behind her, I was ready to question Misty as to where she was and what she was doing when she heard the crash. While she thought about it, I paced about the kitchen, in the style of Alyx's favorite detective, Agatha Christie's Hercule Poirot. I stopped in front of her, and my whiskers twitched involuntarily as I listened to her story.

She recalled bit by bit that she was in the guestroom, reclining on the back of the wicker daybed watching the silly squirrels chase each other up and down trees, insinuating that cats would never waste their time in such trivial pursuit. She was sure that she saw Ethan's car in the driveway but when she went to the front door, it was gone. She went back to the guestroom and when she heard the crash, she saw Pooky running down the hall but didn't see where she went.

The part about seeing Ethan's car in the driveway was disturbing. As Misty suggested, it was possible that he realized he forgot something and left, but what if someone saw his car, and didn't see him leave without getting out of the car. The thought made it more important than ever to bring Pooky in and find out what she knew. I didn't want to jump to the wrong conclusion, so it was important that I convince Pooky to come in, if she didn't do it on her own. My thinking revolved around the fact that there had to be a reason why Pooky ran away. She had spent two horrible weeks outdoors and nearly died when her humans abandoned her, it didn't make sense that she would go back out there.

Eager to pin something on Pooky, Misty remembered that before the loud noise, she saw Pooky making her way to the kitchen, chasing after something, adding that maybe Pooky was the one responsible for what happened to Alyx. Didn't I see her running from the kitchen when I heard the crash? True, but Misty was right behind her, I noted. Also true, Misty contributed; she rarely jumped on anything higher than three feet.

I thought it best to let Misty know that I was going to try to talk Pooky into coming back in the house. Misty didn't understand how that was going to happen with the door locked. I awed her to the point of embarrassment on my part when she learned that I knew how to unlock the cat door, and that Maggie had propped open the outside screen door. I explained my strategy, and she gladly agreed to stand guard and alert me if she saw any sign of Pooky while I slept in preparation for my outdoor adventure.

I believed my mother when she told me that according to legend, the *M* on my forehead was the mark of the gods. That had to mean something. Mother also told me about the great gift given to all cats—nine lives. This, I understood, was to reassure me that if I ever ended up in one of those so called *humane* places, where most animals never came out of, I would be courageous and not lose hope. Personally, I was happy with my first life and didn't particularly care to find out if there was a second.

I slid the latch over with my paw and was quickly out on the screened porch. Just a few steps and I cautiously slipped out the screen door, crouching low. I leaped blithely in the air and disappeared into the tall ferns surrounding the small brick patio just outside the door.

When I landed in the ferns, my natural instincts took over, and my vision immediately adjusted to the darkness of the moonless night. The gnarled branches of the live oak trees took on a menacing appearance, the lush landscaping in daytime was a jungle at night, and I was no longer a domestic house cat; I was a wild jungle cat.

Since I had prepared for the task, I wasn't afraid, even though it was my first venture outside after dark. A firm believer in the adage, "Hope for the best, and prepare for the worst," I had anticipated my fears; having seen raccoons in the backyard from time to time, and heard the frightening noises they made fighting each other. I was also fully aware of the stray cats that occasionally roamed the yard. But most important, I was confident of my abilities; I felt I had overcome the handicap of not having any front claws. I had sharpened my skills using my back feet for fighting by practicing on Misty. Still—I hoped I would not have to fight.

There were shadows and noises all around me as I stealthily made my way to where I thought Pooky was hiding. I recognized two sounds: the hooting of the great horned owls in the distance, and the whining of a screech owl—a tremulous descending wail coming from right above me where the bird made its home in the cavity of an old tree. Owls are nocturnal hunters and fearless in defense of their nest and it was unsettling when I looked up and she turned her head the full range of her ability. I was prepared to defend myself but sensed she was no threat, just curious.

Pooky was nearby, I sensed it; but she stayed out of sight. In fact, I knew exactly where she was and could have pounced on her at any time, but since I didn't intend to hurt her, I didn't want to chance her running out of the yard. I let her know that Alyx had been hurt, that she was alive but in a coma and that Ethan had been arrested for trying to kill her, and needed help to prove his innocence.

To my consternation, she stubbornly remained hidden. I sat for a long time, all the while explaining how important it was for me to know exactly what had happened Saturday morning. I let her know that the doors were open, there was food and water in the lanai if she decided to do what she knew was right. My last plea was to remind her that Alyx had saved her life and deserved her help. On that note, I cautiously headed back to the house. The moon continued to hide but it didn't matter, I could see just as well without the moonlight.

It felt good to be outside; the freedom was exhilarating. My senses heightened; I stopped abruptly and crouched to leap. Someone else had entered the yard—several others, in fact.

Suddenly, a scruffy, gray cat brazenly stepped directly in my path, making loud, guttural, screeching noises as if I was the one trespassing rather than the other way around.

I immediately recognized him as the bully often seen hanging around the yard when no one was home. I answered with a few choice words of my own and stood my ground—fur puffed up, ears back, crouched low to the ground, and ready to spring, if necessary.

Engaged in a stare-down match with the stray, I heard rustling noises in the bushes and caught flashes of fur, alerting me to the stray's friends gathering around for the fight. At the same time, there was another sound behind and to my left, between me and the other cats. In my peripheral vision, I saw Pooky surreptitiously making her way towards me. I let out a low growl, warning her to stay out of it. To my right, I heard Misty pawing at the screen, itching to get out. I had enough to worry about and hoped they would both stay put.

Clearly aware of my handicap, I knew I had to act quickly. Letting out a surprisingly loud screech, I leaped into action, my clawless paws smacking the gray cat into confusion. I pounced like a football player defending the last touchdown and quickly had the cat pinned down on its back. Having no claws, I had to rely on teeth and back legs, biting the cat's neck repeatedly while shredding his stomach with my back feet.

The quickness of my actions had the cat disoriented. I savored the win, and then slowly released my hold. The intruder started to back off but not before taking one last swipe, catching me on the nose with his claws. I wanted to tear him up but allowed him to run away, as all bullies do when confronted.

When I was sure the intruder and his friends were all out of the yard, I made my way back inside. Misty rubbed against me, checking for injuries. She licked the gash on my nose, and inspected the chunks of missing fur on my ears.

"Prowling his own quiet backyard or asleep by the fire, he is still only a whisker away from the wilds."
– Jean Burden

CHAPTER FOURTEEN: *A Ploy Well Played*

Curled up tight, paws over my eyes, tail wrapped around myself securely, I winced slightly as I uncurled and saw Misty looking down on me from her perch on the back of my chair. Arching my back first, and then stretching languidly and yawning, I reminded her that, according to cat etiquette, it wasn't proper to stare. I was hungry and headed for the kitchen, happy to see there was enough food and water for breakfast. When I finished, I approached Misty with an idea I had worked out during the night when it looked like I was sleeping. She quickly agreed, without questioning my instructions, to watch for Pooky and to report to me if she saw her come in, and do absolutely nothing else— strongly emphasizing the latter, explaining that I didn't want anything to scare Pooky away.

I was sure that Pooky had the answer, and if I could get her to tell me what happened, I was certain I would be able to communicate it to an appropriate human.

Misty was on duty at her post in front of one of the tall windows looking out to the back yard, not moving a muscle. Maggie walked past her and came to me curled up in a ball on Alyx's bed. When she called me, I opened one eye briefly, but didn't move.

"What's the matter, Murfy? You miss Alyx, don't you?" she asked as she inspected the slash on my nose and the tufts of fur missing around my ears.

"What happened to you, fur-baby? You look like you've been in a fight. I told you the other day not to mess with Misty or someone was going to get hurt, and it looks like Misty won. Come on; let's get you something special to eat."

The police were through with their investigation, and the yellow tape closing off the kitchen was gone. Maggie opened my favorite can of food and emptied it on a paper plate. I just collapsed in front of it, stretching out my front paws, placing my chin flat between them, giving the impression that I was sad and depressed.

The ploy worked. She joined me on the floor. "Ethan is all right," she said reassuringly. "His Dad's been to see him, and he hired David Hunter, the best defense lawyer in the county who's working hard on his case."

She shook her head and ruffled my fur. "Listen to me," she said. "I must be losing my grip on reality. I'm actually talking to a cat."

Nevertheless, she continued to talk, saying not to worry, Alyx was fine, and she would be home soon. "Before you know it; your family will be back."

I couldn't exactly say she was lying, but she wasn't telling me everything either. Earlier that day, I had overheard Mrs. Leary tell a neighbor in the backyard that they had charged Ethan with first-degree attempted murder, denied him bail, and transferred him to the County Branch Jail.

Maggie then commented on the fact that according to the wife of the judge who had denied Ethan's bail, Judge Terrence Stoner, a pillar of the community and due to retire in four months, her husband wanted nothing to mar his record. The rumor was that Judge Stoner had been elected to err on the side of caution. He had concluded that Ethan was financially irresponsible, emotionally unstable and could be a danger to his mother.

As far as I could tell, the only good news was that Bob Hille had hired a good defense attorney. He had finally come through for his son—being there when Ethan needed him.

Always a gentleman, I ate my portion and then relieved Misty at her post so she could share the special treat. Maggie, in the meantime, took care of our other needs. A while later, I heard her tell someone on the phone that she was heading to the hospital. I thought about hitching a ride, making sure that she didn't see me this time, but decided to walk instead. Measuring the journey a*s the crow flies*; it was a shorter distance.

"It is in the nature of cats to do a certain amount of unescorted roaming."—Adlai Stevenson

CHAPTER FIFTEEN: *The Awakening*

Maggie must have taken a detour. She wasn't at the hospital when I arrived. I found out I wasn't heavy enough to open the automatic doors and I had to wait for someone who was. I picked two teen girls, both busy talking on their phones, confident they wouldn't notice me slide in behind them. After that, I had to be careful, ducking behind open doors and corners.

Just as I arrived in her room, the monitors were blinking wildly, and several medical staff members hurried into the room. Alyx sat up with a jolt. I ducked behind a screen near the door, and peeked out so I could hear and see everything that happened.

Dr. Casey introduced himself to Alyx and asked her if she knew where she was, where she lived, and what year she was born. He explained that they would be doing a lot of testing to make sure everything was functioning as it should. Luckily, I went unnoticed in all the confusion,

A bit later, Alyx's ex-husband Bob, Detective Smarts and his partner walked in and took a stand at the foot of the bed. Behind the drawn curtain, I could hear Alyx ask the nurse taking her vitals if she could have something for her headache.

"This dreadful headache is making it impossible for me to string two thoughts together; they disappear as quickly as they come. Why am I here?"

"You were hit on the head and have been in a coma for two days."

The nurse pulled open the curtain around the bed Alyx looked confused, and for a moment, the confusion rendered her silent. She glanced to her left hand, probably to confirm that she wasn't married to Bob anymore. Perplexed, she turned to him for an explanation, and he said he'd explain later.

Smarts stepped up to her bedside. "Are you Alyx Hille?"

"Yes, I am."

"I'm Detective Smarts, Beachside Police, and this is my partner, Detective Albright."

Albright nodded his acknowledgement.

"Ms. Hille, do you know why you're here?"

She brought two fingers to her temple in a useless gesture, as it didn't seem to ease her pain.

"Yes, the nurse told me I was hit on the head."

"Can you tell me what you remember about Saturday morning?"

At that moment, Doctor Casey came back into the room and interceded on her behalf.

"Excuse me, Detective Smarts. I understand it's your job to ask questions, but Ms. Hille's not ready to be questioned, and I'll have to ask you to do it another time."

"All right; but can I just ask one question before we go?"

"One question and only one."

The detective turned back to Alyx. "Did you see who hit you?"

She shook her head and shrugged. "The last thing I remember is sitting at the kitchen table, then sudden blinding pain followed by an abyss of darkness."

"Thank you, Ms. Hille; we'll talk again when your doctor gives his permission."

Bob stepped back as the others left, but he didn't go out; then he stood in the doorway for a moment as if he didn't want whoever was out there to see him. Alyx waited for the room to empty, before she asked, "So why are you here, Bob?"

He shifted from one foot to the other. "I'm not staying long. You have other company here to see you."

"Did something happen to Ethan? Why are you here instead of him?"

"Ethan is fine...but...Alyx, I don't know how else to say this other than just say it. He's not here because he's been arrested for attempted murder."

Her body went limp so she could barely speak. "Attempted murder of whom?"

"You."

"Happy owner, happy cat. Indifferent owner, reclusive cat."—
Chinese Proverb

CHAPTER SIXTEEN: *Guilty Until Proven Innocent*

"You're joking, right?"

"I wish I was, but no; I'm not joking"

"I don't know whether to laugh or cry. That's unbelievable. How did they arrive at that conclusion?"

"His lawyer, David Hunter, says the evidence against him is substantial."

"I'm sorry; I'm having trouble processing what you're saying. Did you say Ethan has been arrested for trying to kill me?"

They stopped talking when Maggie entered the room in a whirlwind and went straight to Alyx's bedside. "He told you, didn't he?"

The animosity was palpable between Bob and Maggie, as always. Bob said he had an appointment with Ethan's lawyer and that he'd be back later to check on her and left in a hurry, almost stepping on my tail which was dangling a bit under the screen, as he stormed out of the room.

"He's got a lot of nerve," snarled Maggie.

"Maggie, it's okay," replied Alyx. "He said Ethan asked him to keep an eye on me."

"I know; Ethan told me he was going to do that. He's worried that since the police think they have their man, they've stopped looking and whoever wanted to hurt you is still out there."

"Well, then give him a break, Maggie. I know you don't like him. I know you think he's a jackass for his emotional abandonment of Ethan, and I agree, but he's trying to make up for it. After all, he did hire the attorney for Ethan's defense. The 'best in the county,' meaning he didn't come cheap."

"Yeah, well...that wasn't exactly his idea," Maggie said in a hushed tone. "I knew you'd be mad when you found out," then louder, "but that man has had an easy ride for too long."

"He didn't know I was struggling to make ends meet while Ethan finished college. I never asked him for financial support. And I'm not mad. You had no choice; you got stuck with the store, the clients, and the cats." She took a deep breath and let it out. "I don't want to talk about Bob anymore."

"Okay, let's not talk about Bob. What's important is how you are?"

"They tell me I'm going to be all right; vision, hearing, and motor skills are a little sluggish, but are all working properly. I do have a horrible headache that they tell me will go away, eventually. Dr. Casey wants to keep me in the hospital for a few more days but I'm going to try to get him to discharge me tomorrow."

Maggie didn't comment.

"I had the strangest experience just before I opened my eyes."

"You remember it? That's incredible."

"I found myself in a strange state of being. It was as if I was dreaming, but not exactly. There were split second occurrences when I felt my eyelids flicker as if given an electric charge. At first, it was just sparks of awareness, sparks that gradually spread to other areas of the brain. The sensation was that of falling asleep, that instant when consciousness gives way to unconsciousness, that place that I sometimes feel pulled to and fight to come back from, waking with a start— heart pounding.

I heard a voice and felt the warmth of a touch. Focusing on that sensation seemed to boost my ability to pull out of the darkness. Then, it ended, thrusting me into an odd twilight zone where I struggled to understand the nebulous images forming in my mind.

I saw myself as a young woman in my parents' living room. There were colored lights and pleasant sounds. The sounds were familiar voices. The colored lights swimming in front of me organized into a continuous string wrapped around a Christmas tree.

The dream was pleasant and I didn't want to wake up. I saw my brother with a movie camera; his wife was directing the action. She told everyone to get up and dance. "Try to look like you're having fun," she said. Everyone got up and pretended to dance, pretended because there was no music, and laughed for real.

That scene faded into darkness, and another picture emerged. It didn't take as long to recognize the house that Bob and I lovingly renovated right after we got married. I was looking down at the beautiful, angelic face of a baby boy—our baby. Bob had his arm loosely draped around my shoulders, and cold as steel, his empty blue eyes cut through me to the core. I could feel my heart thudding. I fought to wake up from the nightmare, but descended into a deeper darkness instead. Suddenly, another scene emerged. This time, I was sitting on the couch with an arm around a ten-year-old boy who was crying softly while his father was trying to explain why he was moving somewhere else. Overcome with unbelievable sadness for the boy, I felt real tears streaming down my cheeks, the sadness turned to anger, and that's when I woke-up."

"You should write it all down before you forget it."

"That's why I told you. I learned that if I tell someone my dreams as soon as I wake up, I don't forget them, and since you recorded it, I won't forget for sure."

"You gave us quite a scare, sweetie. I'm glad you're going to be all right. I know Ethan will be happy to hear the news; he's been worried about you."

"And I'm worried about him. I didn't see anyone or hear anything before I was hit in the head, Saturday morning," she said, trying hard not to sound hopeless. "All I know is that I was sitting at the kitchen table waiting for you and Ethan, and the next thing, I'm in a hospital bed." Her voice broke and she pulled a tissue from the box on her side table.

"Maggie," Alyx said, "I'm sure Ethan didn't do this. It's so unfair. By keeping him in prison, they are punishing him without a trial. What ever happened to innocent until proven guilty?"

"I know what you mean. I guess the judge looked at the evidence and decided Ethan could be a threat to you, or could leave town or both."

"Ethan wouldn't have done either of those things because he's innocent," Alyx asserted in frustration.

Just then, a young man about Ethan's age, wearing khakis, a black shirt and a striped blue, yellow and navy tie walked in.

"Ms. Hille, my name is Tony…Tony Mallory. I'm an investigator from the State Attorney's office. I'd like to ask you some questions."

Maggie got up to leave. Alyx put her hand out signaling her to stay. "Is it okay if my friend stays?"

"No problem, if that's what you want."

Maggie sat back down while Alyx told the young investigator the same story she had told Smarts and Maggie.

Then, the young man showed Alyx pictures of the pieces of pottery found on the kitchen floor. I stretched my head out from behind the screen, trying to catch a glimpse of the photos. "Just one more question, Ms. Hille. Here is a photograph of the presumed weapon used, the earthenware pot; do you recognize it? Do you remember where it was?"

"I'm sorry," replied Alyx, "I still feel a little disoriented. I can't quite picture it or where it might have been displayed." She lay back on the hospital bed.

"Is this necessary? Can't you come back tomorrow?" questioned Maggie.

"It's all right, Maggie," said Alyx, sitting up, "just let me focus for a moment. Ethan made several pots and I have them all over the house. Right now, I have no idea. All I see is pieces of a broken pot." She shook her head in discouragement.

"Dogs have owners, cats have staff."—Unknown

CHAPTER SEVENTEEN: *Sentimental Expressions*

She couldn't muster any enthusiasm for it, but Alyx agreed to Maggie's offer to read her get-well cards and the gift tags on the flowers, no doubt to cheer her up, although, she didn't say so.

I saw Alyx wipe away an errant tear. "Since I rarely hear from anyone, I'm surprised and touched by all the cards and flowers from my family. I was always the one to initiate contact, and when I stopped calling, no one else picked up the phone. At first, I excused it by telling myself they were just busy, caught up in their own lives and families, but I was busy too and somehow I managed to find the time. After a while, I just didn't think about it at all. As you know, the only one that keeps in touch with me is my older sister, Kathy, and that's only a few times a year, usually around the holidays."

"I think they mean the sentiments expressed in these cards, don't you?" Maggie asked.

"Yes, I do and when this mess is straightened out, I'm going home for a visit, and I'd like you to come. Ethan too, if he can take off work," Alyx said with resolve.

"It's a deal," Maggie said as she picked up a colorful watering can filled with daisies. "I think these are my favorite. They're so cheerful."

"You know how much I love flowers; they're all beautiful to me. Who sent those?"

"Charvette said they're from Justin Marks, the dealer you met at the antique show in Georgia—the guy you never mentioned to me."

"I never mentioned him because there was nothing to mention. We had coffee a couple of times and then we lost track of him. Why is he sending me flowers?" Alyx said.

Maggie opened the gift tag and looked up puzzled. "That's weird; there's no name on the card. How did Charvette know who sent them?" she questioned. "It just says 'I wish you a peaceful rest.' That's a strange thing to say, don't you think?"

Alyx wasn't paying attention, didn't answer her question, and asked one of her own instead, "Do they allow prisoners to make calls whenever they want?"

"Not whenever. They have certain times when they can make calls. I'm sure Ethan will call as soon as he can, once he knows you're awake."

"Can I call him?"

"No; they're not allowed to receive calls and they can only make collect calls out." Alyx looked around, dazed and leaned back on the bed. "Alyx, you're starting to fade out. I'm going to take off so you can get some rest. Is there anything you want me to bring you from home when I come back?"

Alyx appeared to think about it, and then asked for a few things: toothbrush, hairbrush, lipstick and mascara, and some bedclothes that didn't expose her to the world. She pulled the cover up to her neck while Maggie gathered her things and was asleep before Maggie left the room.

Maggie didn't say where she was going, and if she went home and didn't find me there, I'd have a big problem on my hands. I faced a dilemma. When Bob had left, he said he was going to see David Hunter, and I heard him on the phone out in the hall making an appointment to meet him at an outdoor coffee shop within walking distance of the hospital. It was important that I know exactly what was going on with Ethan from the lawyer's point of view and also ascertain if Alyx was in any danger. I started to think maybe I'd made a mistake by thinking I could handle it all. I quickly dismissed that negative thought and decided to take a chance with Maggie. I still had an hour before Bob's appointment with the lawyer and decided to stay where I was for the time being.

Alyx was lying with her back to the door, so she didn't see anyone come in, and didn't know anyone was in the room until she heard whispering. Her brother Tom and his wife Susan had entered and were at her side.

"I'm sorry; I didn't know you were here."

Tom squeezed her hand. "Glad to see you're awake."

"We thought you were sleeping and didn't want to wake you," chimed in Susan.

"I've been awake for a while. I was trying hard to remember anything that might shed some light on what happened. There's something tickling the back of my mind and it just isn't coming to the surface. How long have you been here?"

"We've been sitting out in the hall for about ten minutes or so."

"We were here yesterday too," said Susan as she leaned down to kiss Alyx's cheek. "Anyway, how do you feel?"

"Physically, I'm fine. Hopefully, I'll be able to go home tomorrow."

"Ethan called and left a message but the message didn't say much about what had happened and he didn't have anything to add when we came to see you Saturday," said Tom.

"I think he was embarrassed that we caught him holding your hand and talking to you when we walked in," said Susan. I told him I thought it was a good idea, that maybe you could hear him and help you find your way home. He just gave me a tight-lipped smile."

"So, what happened? Did you see who hit you?" asked Tom.

Susan interrupted, "What about the police, do they know who might have done this or why?" and at the same time, Tom wanted to know what she remembered.

Susan shook her head. "Very strange situation, if you ask me."

Although they had moved to Florida a few years before Alyx's divorce and only lived thirty miles away, they hadn't been there for Alyx when she needed support nor had they played a big role in Ethan's life while he was growing up. In fact, Alyx hardly ever saw them and her reaction to the intrusive and irritating rapid fire questioning, was what I expected.

"This is starting to sound like an inquisition," and she quickly added, "I'm sorry; I didn't mean that the way it came out."

"Yes you did," Tom stated, "and you're right." He turned to Susan, "We should go. She needs to rest," he said as he took her hand.

Alyx followed their hesitant exit from the room, the sense of loss reflected in the expression on her face. I wondered if they knew that Ethan was in jail; they hadn't mentioned it, so maybe they didn't, but it didn't matter; they probably wouldn't visit him anyway.

Both Alyx and Ethan liked to bring me along when they went on their errands so I knew my way around downtown, logically more so my own neighborhood. The sidewalk café where Bob was to meet the defense attorney had several large potted plants to hide behind, one close enough for me to hear their conversation.

"She's going behind Alyx's back and using Ethan to boot," were the first words out of Bob's mouth.

"I'm glad you called with the information," Hunter said after they shook hands.

"I knew she couldn't be trusted. I told Alyx the first time I met her that she was too good to be true. "

Hunter pulled out a notebook from his briefcase and placed it on the table. "What did you hear, exactly?"

"Maggie said that, no, she didn't get a chance to talk to Alyx again about the offer, and she said that Alyx was still mad at her for even considering moving the store to another location."

"What about Ethan, how is he involved?"

"Maggie said that she hadn't asked Ethan if he'd discussed it with his mother."

David Hunter leaned back in his chair, took a deep breath, and exhaled through pursed lips.

"I took this case because I believe Ethan is innocent. I knew from the start that it was going to be a challenge. We all hoped his mother could clear him but now you tell me she doesn't remember anything." He pinched the bridge on his nose. "I don't suppose you have any aspirin, do you?"

"No, my wife usually carries that stuff in her purse."

"As I said, I believe Ethan is innocent, the prosecutor believes it's an open and shut case and the evidence supports it. I'm afraid nothing short of a miracle is going to keep that young man out of prison. At this point, the only defense is to emphasize the good relationship between Ethan and his mother. The jury has to be convinced that he could not have committed the crime."

The server brought two iced coffees, placed them both in front of Hunter, and handed one to Bob.

"Frankly, I'm having a tough time finding anything positive for Ethan," noted the lawyer, "and depending on what he has to say, what you've just told me may turn out to hurt him rather than help."

Bob's face registered confusion followed by disappointment. "How can it hurt him? It sounds to me like Maggie had a motive for wanting Alyx out of the way."

"That's true. She may have had a motive and opportunity, but so did Ethan, and it's his prints on the pot," he stated. "I'm sorry; I know that's not what you want to hear."

"No. I understand. I don't like it, but I understand."

"At any rate, I'm going to see Ethan some time today. I'll discuss it with him and I'll take it from there. I'll also tell him the good news that his mother has regained consciousness, and then I have to tell him the bad news that she doesn't know who hit her."

David Hunter then told Bob that he was going to interview Alyx next, and in my zeal to get back to Alyx's room before he did, I sprinted and accidently bumped into the next table, knocking an empty plastic cup off the table—I'm pretty sure Hunter saw me running away—if only my backside.

"I love little pussy, her coat is so warm, and if I don't hurt her she'll do me no harm."—Mother Goose rhyme

CHAPTER EIGHTEEN: *A Morning Like Any Other Morning*

At the hospital, I was back at my post behind the screen in Alyx's room. As I peeked out her doorway, I saw David Hunter stopped at the nurse's station, apparently asking the charge nurse if Alyx was well enough to interview.

"Dr. Casey's instructions are that she can do what she's able to, so let's go to her room and see if she's up to it," I could hear the nurse say.

As the lawyer followed the nurse to Alyx's room, I quickly sneaked behind the screen again—just in time. Hunter walked through the doorway behind the nurse who strode directly toward the bed. Raccoon eyes looked up when the nurse gently touched Alyx's arm. Her short brown hair was flat in the back, bangs sticking out in front, but she didn't seem to care.

"There's a David Hunter here to see you. Are you up to answering some questions?"

At first, Alyx looked at the man blankly.

"I'm Ethan's attorney, Ms. Hille."

When she realized who he was, she brought her bed up to a sitting position and told the nurse that, yes, she'd be glad to speak to him. "I saw you on the news, the day someone sent me into oblivion. I liked what you said."

Hunter inquired after her health and started right in.

"Before you tell me exactly what happened, I want you to think back to a few days before you were hit. Did you see anyone loitering around your house or your store? Anyone or anything that gave you pause?"

Alyx closed her eyes and slowly shook her head. I was worried about my human. She looked so tired.

"All right, now think carefully and tell me what happened Saturday morning before you blacked out. Tell me everything you saw or heard, no matter how unimportant a detail. What you might think routine may be a clue for me."

Alyx took a deep breath. "I was up early. I made a pot of coffee and went out to get the paper. I put the breakfast items I needed on the counter, and sat at the kitchen table to read the paper while waiting for Ethan and Maggie to show up. I'd called them the night before and invited them over for breakfast...I owed Maggie an apology. I had reacted very badly to her suggestion that we should discuss the offer to sell our building and move Antiques & Designs somewhere else. And I had asked Ethan to come over because I wanted to talk to him about his spending habits in a calmer way than I had previously done—this time I had some concrete suggestions to offer." She leaned over for a sip of the water sitting on the bed tray. "I didn't see or hear anyone come in. That's all I know, until I woke up here."

"Did you leave the door unlocked when you went out for the paper?"

She gave it some thought. "I don't know."

"Okay. You were sitting at the table; maybe you looked out your window; what did you see?"

She closed her eyes again. "No, nothing. There was no one out there."

"All right; let's try it again. You were sitting at the table, the paper in front of you; you took a sip of coffee. What did you hear?"

"I was alone. I didn't have the radio or television on. The cats were being cats. You know, chasing around the house, jumping on things." She rubbed her forehead. "I'm sorry. There's just nothing there—I don't know if I don't remember or there's nothing to remember."

"Are you sure you didn't see or hear a car come up your drive?" he asked.

"No, but I did get up from the table at one point. I heard scratching noises in the guestroom; I looked in and saw one of the cats trying to keep from falling off the back of the wicker day bed. She's a little clumsy at times," she added with a smile.

"Someone could have driven up then and you wouldn't have heard or seen them, right?"

"No, I guess not, but I was just in the doorway for a minute. Why is this important?"

Before he answered, he squinted and rubbed his forehead. "Earlier today, I received a call from the Prosecutor. He said a witness had come forward, a neighbor down the street. He said he stepped outside to get his paper and he saw an SUV the same make and color your son drives, backing out of your drive about ten minutes before your son said he arrived." I felt my fur rise when I heard this.

Alyx too seemed to tremble at the import of that accusation. "I stand by what I said. My son is innocent; he would never hurt me or anyone else for that matter. Please help him," she implored, her eyes clouded, and she tried hard not to lose control.

David Hunter covered her hand with his and then abruptly removed it. "I believe Ethan is innocent and I will do the best I can for him." He cleared his throat and continued, "You said you were going to speak to Ethan about his financial situation. Did you typically argue a lot about his spending habits?"

She shook her head. "I knew he was making good money and for the first time in a long time, Ethan could buy what he wanted as well as just what he needed. Although he didn't discuss his finances with me, I did caution him about the credit card trap he could easily fall into, but every time I brought it up, he told me not to worry; he knew what he was doing. I thought he should make his own decisions, and I didn't press him. I didn't know how deep in debt he was until recently. As for arguments, we never really argued about anything; we had parent-adult child disagreements over his spending."

"Did he ever ask you for money?"

"No, Ethan never asked me for anything. He learned at an early age that I could provide for our needs, but not necessarily for what he wanted."

She smiled wistfully. "Whenever he asked for something, I would ask him if it was a want or a need. Most times, the poor baby would lower his head and tell me he just wanted it. It broke my heart when I had to tell him no. I couldn't be too hard on him about his spending. I knew he was trying to fulfill all those wants he had missed, those things I couldn't give him."

"What about his break-up with his longtime girlfriend? I understand he went through some serious depression."

She took a deep breath. "Yes, it hurt him deeply and I suggested he see a doctor. I thought a he could give him something to help him through it, and it did."

Hunter then showed her a picture of what the reassembled broken pot looked like. "This is the pot you were presumably hit with; do you recognize it?"

She looked at it carefully. "I have the pots Ethan made in high school all over the house—a mother's pride, you know. This one was right above where I was sitting, close to the edge on the upper cabinets."

"I'd like to take another look at the crime scene. Who should I contact?"

"Maggie can let you in. I'll let her know to expect your call."

"Does she have a key to your house?"

"Yes, she does. I gave it to her when I went to a show in Georgia, and I haven't asked for it back. I think I just forgot about it."

"Tell me about Maggie."

"Maggie is my closest friend and business partner. She wouldn't have had anything to do with this."

"I'm not saying she did, Ms. Hille; this is part of the discovery process. I'll be speaking to her as well as others."

"Okay, I understand. I met Maggie when I was taking design classes at Beachside Community College. We found we had a lot in common, even though she doesn't have any children or pets, is twice married and, as she often says, has been burned in love more times than she cares to admit.

We both worked a number of meaningless jobs for large homogenizing institutions that didn't recognize individual effort and achievement. She understood what it takes for an older woman to succeed in a man's world dominated by youth. We often talked about owning our own business and not having to depend on anyone to take care of us.

I encouraged her to stay in school when it became too heavy a load and she wanted to quit, not realizing at the time that what I had said to her was also strengthening my resolve to change my life for the better. You could say our friendship was the crutch that kept us both on the path to a secure future.

Our dream was finally realized when we opened Antiques, each contributing our own unique style and talent to the endeavor. Her concept of a casual atmosphere; no pressure to buy, yet finding assistance nearby if needed and my idea that the store should look like someone's home, so the customer could easily imagine how a particular item would fit in the room they were decorating is what made the store an overnight success. Two months ago, we hired two employees—Charvette and Bernice—giving us the opportunity to develop the interior design part of the business.

Our first job came about when an older couple, who had recently moved down from New Jersey, bought the first house built on the beachside in 1884 to restore it to a bed-and-breakfast. The couple came to Antiques to look for furnishings for their own home and liked our decorating style. They hired us to decorate the B & B after its completion, but as it turned out, we ended up assisting with many elements of the restoration.

Maggie suggested that the owners host an open house and invite the press. The event turned into a community affair, with several other historic B & B's taking part, the owners dressed in period costumes and serving authentic turn-of-the-century recipes. Along with the tourists, it seemed like the whole town turned out for the event, resulting in positive exposure and business for Antiques & Designs.

I often wonder where I'd be if I hadn't met Maggie."

I admit I so enjoyed hearing Maggie tell about how she and Alyx and met and started their business that I almost forgot about the seriousness of the present situation.

"All right, Ms. Hille, I don't want to tire you out any more than necessary, but I do have a couple more questions. Are you up to continuing or should I come back?"

"Please call me Alyx, and I'm fine. What else do you want to know?"

"I learned from your son and your business partner, that there was resentment against you on the part of some of your neighboring business owners," he said, repeating what Maggie and Ethan had told him. "Do you think any of them would want to hurt you?"

She bit her lower lip and looked away. "I don't know. No, I really don't think so."

"What about Dan Ramsey?"

"I think Dan Ramsey is more envious of our influence over the other merchants, than he is resentful of the changes Maggie and I suggested. Before Antiques moved in, everything closed down at five in the evening and on Sundays. It took Maggie and me three months to convince the Downtown Merchants Association to see the wisdom of extending their daily hours and staying open seven days a week. The resistance came mostly from the merchants who regarded their business as a hobby rather than a business. Some still resent the change, the most vocal being Dan Ramsey. Judging from his outburst at the Merchant's Association meeting, he looked angry enough to want to kill me, but I don't think it was him."

"Either one—jealousy or resentment—can be a motive for murder," Hunter said as he pulled a business card from his coat pocket and wrote his home phone number on the back.

"If you remember anything else, anything at all, call my office, my cell phone or my home if it's after business hours."

"If there is a trial, what are Ethan's chances?"

"At this point, the prosecution's case is strong. No doubt, they will, bring up the fact that Ethan needed cash to keep up with his acquired tastes. They will press the issue that he stood to gain the most by the sale of the building, and that he tried to kill you because you wouldn't sell, or maybe your arguing just got out of hand. If he's found guilty, he could receive the minimum of three years. There's always a chance he could be found not guilty—there's also the possibility he could receive a life sentence."

"I don't want to put you on the spot, but I'd like to be kept in the loop regarding Ethan's defense. However, I do understand that, officially, my ex-husband Bob is your client, and you don't have to tell me anything."

He hesitated and looked away before answering her silent plea.

"I give Bob a transcribed copy of all my interviews; I'll be glad to ask for his authorization to give you a copy as well."

Alyx smiled and reached for his hand. "Thank you."

"For a good cat, a good rat."—French Proverb

CHAPTER NINETEEN: *Antiques, Tours, and Interviews*

It had been a while since I'd last been downtown and the walk down Ocean Street gave me the opportunity to reacquaint myself with the area. The renovation of the business area had been completed and the main street was now home to antique stores, art galleries, unique boutiques, and quaint sidewalk cafés. The buildings were mostly art deco style, recently repainted in various shades of beige, aqua and pink, colorful canopies topping the doors and windows.

I had learned from a report that Ethan did in college that the 1910 bank building I passed housed a museum, and just down the street, where the residential area began, the Live Oak House dating back to 1700 overlooked the marina. Four hundred years old, live oak trees surrounded the current house built in 1871; the original structure having burned down during the second Seminole Indian War. Also in the heart of the old downtown area was another registered historic house built in 1912 of coquina limestone created by centuries of transforming sand, shell and coral.

I stopped to look at the display window at Alyx and Maggie's shop, Antiques & Designs, admiring the beautifully crafted desk in excellent condition that was tucked in the corner of the display. I saw David Hunter driving down the street, looking for a parking spot, so I quickly entered the store.

Many of the antique stores that Alyx had taken me to had been either full of stodgy dark antiques, or so full of junk you had to dig your way through to find anything worthwhile. Antiques & Designs was different; here customers found a bright and orderly display of goods set up to look much like the rooms in a lived-in home, the antiques mixed in with vintage furniture. Some of the items evolved from other things with previous lives, such as the corner-shelf created from two louvered bi-fold door panels and the bench that had had a previous life as a headboard.

The space was open with only the furniture delineating the various rooms. Off to the side, towards the middle of the space was a wide, majestic staircase curving up to the loft area on the second floor.

An attractive, flamboyantly-dressed woman in her thirties walked up to Hunter and offered to assist him. "I'm here to see Maggie Broeck. Are you Ms. Broeck?"

"No, I'm Bernice. Maggie is with a customer now. Is there anything I can help you with?" she asked pleasantly. Hunter handed her his business card and told her he just needed to speak to Maggie for a few minutes.

Bernice glanced at the card. "I'll let her know you're here."

He smiled a thank you and watched her disappear up the curving staircase. A few minutes later, Maggie came down the stairs. Attractive in a conventional way, Maggie was dressed in a conservative, turquoise suit. The warm, friendly personality she presented was genuine. She introduced herself and directed Hunter to the office in the rear of the store. I followed unseen.

In contrast to the décor of the store, the office was completely modern-day and functional. Maggie offered Hunter some coffee, which he declined, poured herself a cup and sat behind the desk. He took a seat next to the desk, pulled out a notebook and recorder from his briefcase, and placed the briefcase on the floor, next to his chair.

"How can I help you, Mr. Hunter?"

"Call me David. I'd like to ask you some questions, just to clear up a few points. Do you mind if I record the conversation? You strike me as someone who has a lot to say and I don't take shorthand."

"You're right; I usually do have a lot to say, but not about what happened to Alyx. I have no idea who or why someone would want to hurt her."

"I understand. My questions, however, are about you. I know you have access to the house, but your statement to the police makes no mention of it. Why didn't you tell them you have a key?"

She looked down. "I don't know. I'm not good at analyzing my actions. I did tell Ethan I'd be taking care of the cats and the house. I assumed he understood I had a key. If I had anything to hide I wouldn't have done that."

David Hunter had his questions written down and moved on to number two.

"Alyx's ex-husband Bob Hille overheard a conversation you were having on the phone outside of Alyx's hospital room."

I watched Maggie closely for a reaction. A look of disdain crossed her face at the mention of Bob's name. She essentially said that she had been surprised at Alyx's reaction about moving the business and had enlisted Ethan to help.

"Who was the realtor who contacted you?"

"His name is Rupert Moresby. His wife, Novie, owns the Ocean Street Café, next door to our business, as a matter of fact."

"Did you discuss the offer with her?"

"Yes, I did. Rupert mentioned that the developer, James Dunne, was also interested in buying the building where the café is located. I wanted to see what Novie's feelings were about selling. I got the impression Rupert wanted it to happen more than she did."

Hunter flipped his notebook to another page. "Ethan mentioned there was some resentment on the part of some of the business owners regarding being pressured to expand their business hours. Can you give more background on that?"

"Ethan and I talked about that before his arrest. He asked me if I knew of anyone who might have wanted to hurt Alyx. I told him I didn't know of any problems among the people we knew, and he reminded me about a nasty confrontation with Dan Ramsey a couple of months back. His store is two doors north," she said, indicating the direction with her head.

"Where did this happen?"

She took a sip of coffee. "It happened at our regular Merchant's Association meeting. Alyx and I presented the idea that it would benefit all of us to get involved in sponsoring community events such as the annual Arts Festival, taking the opportunity to show off our beautiful renovated downtown. Well, he stood up, got all red in the face and, directing his comments to Alyx, said he was tired of *pushy* newcomers changing the order of things. And we heard again about how long he and some of the others had been downtown and had gotten along just fine."

"How did Alyx react to that?"

Maggie grinned. "She stood up, rested both hands on the table in front of her, and told Dan Ramsey that change was inevitable whether he liked it or not, but if he didn't, he should consider selling so that those interested in developing the area to its full potential could do so without hindrance.

Hunter only smiled, and Maggie continued, "Ramsey was also the most vocal when we approached the group about changing business hours when we first opened our store. He and five or six others are in the minority. Most want the changes; they just didn't know it when the old guard was always running the show," she said, finishing her coffee.

He flipped a few pages back. "What about your employees, Bernice Kustaberry and Charvette Hattaras, anything unusual ever happen between them and Alyx?"

Maggie thought about it. "Nothing I know about. We stole Bernice from the Antique Emporium and Charvette came highly recommended by Novie Moresby next door, whom we know pretty well. Charvette used to work for her husband, Rupert. Although we all like each other and occasionally have lunch, Alyx and I don't socialize with our employees. We prefer to keep things on a business level."

He consulted his notes again. "What about George Lucas? What can you tell me about him?"

"Well, George isn't really an employee," she answered quickly. "He's not on our payroll; we pay him by the piece, whether it's an item he fixed or one he created. Alyx has known him for several years and she's never said anything bad about him nor has he ever said anything bad about her. He's a very talented man and we both feel lucky to have him as a supplier and woodworker."

"I assume that in your business you travel to other cities to find merchandise to sell?"

"Yes, we do, but not very often. I think the last out of town trip was a couple of months ago when Alyx and Charvette went to an antique fair in Georgia, which was when Alyx gave me the key to her house, by the way. She asked me to take care of her cats. She didn't ask for it back when she returned and I just forgot to give it back to her. In fact, it's been here in the drawer of this desk until I took it out Monday," she said.

He made no comment on the key issue and continued his questioning.

"Did anything unusual happen at the fair that you know of? Anything between Charvette and Alyx or someone else?"

She said no. He thanked her for the information and asked if he could speak to Bernice and Charvette.

"Sure, let me go tell them you want to talk to them. I'll ask Bernice to come in first."

"Thank you and I'd also like to speak to George."

"It so happens, I spoke to him a little while ago and he should be here any time."

The interview with Bernice was short, as she didn't have a lot to tell him.

Charvette, conservatively dressed in a navy blue skirt and a light blue sweater set, appeared to be in her late forties, not unattractive but she wouldn't have stood out in a group of women her age. A quiet look of desperation hung over her, though nothing she said or did alluded to that. She was pleasant and eager to answer his questions but didn't have any additional information to add to what we already knew. However, I did notice her hesitance when he asked a routine question about her former employer, Rupert Moresby, in order to establish her background.

That got me thinking. Charvette had been at the hospital shortly after they admitted Alyx. How did she know Alyx was in the hospital? She said she had heard the 911 call go out on some sort of radio, but that wasn't necessarily true. So what was she doing there? And why was she so interested in hearing what Dr.

Casey was saying when she pretended to be looking for something in her purse as an excuse for lingering? Then there was the thing about the flowers. Maggie had caught that but had dismissed it as irrelevant. How did Charvette know who sent the flowers since there was no name on the card?

Maggie told Hunter he was welcome to use the office if he wanted to speak to George and Hunter said he did. She left and, while he waited, he made a call to his assistant. Luckily, I overheard.

"I need you to make a few appointments for me as soon as possible. First, call Maggie Broeck and set up a time when she can meet me at Ms. Hille's house; try for tomorrow. Also, call Rupert Moresby of Moresby Realty, and Novie Moresby, Ocean Street Café, and tell both of them that I'll be stopping by to talk to them in the next two days. Just get a general time frame from them."

"Also," he continued, "call Dan Ramsey, and make an appointment for a specific time, and make it at his convenience. Since you'll be taking a lunch late, take your time coming back."

"I gave an order to a cat, and the cat gave it to its tail."—
Chinese Proverb

CHAPTER TWENTY: *A Crook or Whistle Blower*

Tired and hungry, I was profoundly grateful that Hunter was able to interview George Lucas at Antiques & Designs instead of his home. I had accompanied Alyx to Lucas's house once or twice and I knew that George lived in a rural area outside the city limits. There were a few farms and some homes, mostly on large tracts of land—some large enough to have horses. His house was a modest two-story home with a detached garage and a large shed separate from the house. A long, dirt driveway led to the house, guarded by gigantic Florida pines. The large shed was full of broken furniture, pieces of furniture, lumber and a large inventory of architectural items. In contrast to the shed, the living room was clean, uncluttered, and tastefully decorated. He had told Alyx that very few pieces were authentic—the rest were reissues or reconstructed. Some parts were authentic, some parts not.

Luckily, I did not have to travel so far out today. The two men were settled at one of the antique tables in the front showroom. I listened in from behind a potted palm.

"I read an article in the *Times*," said George, "that said the hot market for modernist furniture is calling into question the authenticity of the pieces as they are rebuilt, repainted, reproduced, or newly assembled. I read that a twentieth-century trestle table sold for over three million dollars. I'd hate to be the owner of that piece and then discover that it wasn't authentic."

Hunter asked him if he used authentic parts to reconstruct the items he sold.

"Yes, I do, but not just with modern pieces, I also do it with antiques and other pieces of furniture."

George quickly provided an explanation.

"Antiques & Designs' customers are fully aware of what they're buying. I put a sticker on the back of each piece I work on, with my signature and an explanation of what was done to the piece."

"Do you have other clients besides Antiques & Designs?" asked the lawyer, checking his ever-present recorder.

"I've had other clients in the past. Lately, I just work for myself—selling at flea markets and shows, and Antiques & Designs."

"Did your other clients disclose the origins of the pieces they sold?"

"I prefer not to answer that, if you don't mind. Buyer beware has always been understood with antiques and it's the same now with modernist furniture."

"How long have you known Alyx?"

"We've run into each other at antique fairs and estate sales for years, and she always made a purchase or two at antique shows and fairs for just as long."

"Do you tell all your customers about the authenticity of your pieces?"

A terse, "Yes, I do," was his answer.

"Do you know anything that might help Ethan's case? Anything you heard or saw that seemed unusual?"

"I regret to say, no."

"What about Antiques & Designs' other employees? Ever hear them discuss any grievances?"

He shook his head. "I never heard them say one derogatory word about Alyx or Maggie. Customers here are treated well and seem to appreciate it, as far as I know."

"Just to make sure I have this right—you and Alyx never argued about making customers aware of the authenticity of the pieces you worked on?"

George stood up. "No, there has never been a question about it, and if you don't mind I have a lot of work to finish."

The interview was obviously over. Hunter turned off the recorder and handed Lucas his card. "It's my job to ask unpleasant questions. Please call me if you have anything to add to our conversation, and thank you for your time."

Hunter received a call from his assistant as George left the room and I gathered from the one-way conversation that Dan Ramsey had agreed to see him on short notice.

"Please would you tell me," said Alice, a little timidly... *"why your cat grins like that."*—Lewis Carroll, *Alice in Wonderland*

CHAPTER TWENTY-ONE: *Important Appointment*

Chaos greeted my entrance. The name of the store was Ramsey's Collectibles—what I saw when I slid through the partially-open back door was junk. The shelves along the walls of the narrow room were overflowing with assorted items that had nothing to do with each other. There were several tables and other pieces of furniture in the middle of the room piled with bulging boxes. Up against one wall, was a small, glass display case filled with small figurines, which I assumed were the collectibles the store name implied.

Hunter entered from the front entrance and scanned the room for signs of life, positioning himself by a display case, which also served as a counter. He asked a clerk to see Dan Ramsey and the un-kept, surly teenager slouching in a chair behind the display case pointed to the *ring for service* bell at the end of the display case. Hunter hit it twice, and Dan Ramsey crawled out from behind a wall in the rear of the store, to my right. Another scruffy-looking youth, older than the one behind the counter, followed him out.

Ramsey was about sixty-years old, heavyset with a full head of white hair, and dark, button eyes. He was dressed in jeans, a loud flowered-shirt, and flip-flops on his feet.

"You must be the lawyer who wanted to see me. I don't get too many people in here dressed in a suit. It makes it too hard to dig through the junk," he chuckled, as he slid behind the counter.

"I appreciate you seeing me so soon, Mr. Ramsey."

"Yeah, well, I figured that someone told you that Alyx Hille and I have our differences—and I don't deny that—but she and that partner of hers have all these hoity-toity ideas about our downtown and they've managed to talk other owners into making unnecessary changes. They've tried to change the essence of Ocean Street, the flavor of the place, and I won't stand for it if I can help it!"

"Do you feel strongly enough about stopping her to want to kill her, maybe?"

The hands in his pockets came out and slammed on the counter. "I agreed to see you, buddy, because I couldn't wait to tell you that on the day in question, I was out of town at a flea market. At least a dozen regular dealers can testify that they saw me there from six in the morning to late afternoon." His eyes narrowed. "And just for the record, I don't know anything about what happened to Ms. Hille—and I can't say I care!" He turned abruptly and went back to the hole behind the wall.

Although, I was truly exhausted, not to mention hungry, I couldn't go home yet.

"In a cat's eye all things belong to cats."—English Proverb

CHAPTER TWENTY-TWO: *A Business Deal*

Although the outside of the building looked like Antiques & Designs, the inside of Ocean Street Café was different. The restaurant took up half of the downstairs, the rest was divided into retail stores—a candle shop, a jewelry store, and a candy store. In square footage, it was roughly twice the size.

Novie Moresby was behind the mahogany checkout counter—I was in the vicinity.

"Mrs. Moresby, I represent Ethan Hille and I have a couple of questions to ask you. I can see you're busy, I'll try to be brief."

"I hope I can help you, but I don't see how. Of course, I know Alyx and Ethan; they used to come in often when they first opened their store and Ethan still lived at home. I see Alyx all the time, but Ethan only occasionally."

"When was the last time you saw them in here?"

"Let's see now. I think they were in here for breakfast about a week ago."

"What kind of relationship did they appear to have?"

"The kind every parent hopes for when they first think about having children. It was obvious they had love and respect for each other."

"Did you ever hear them argue?"

"Not any of the times I saw them together."

"Would you be willing to testify to that?"

"Yes, I certainly would."

"Earlier I spoke to your husband about the real estate proposition he presented to Maggie Broeck. What do you know about it?"

"Just that the Dunne Development Company wants to buy our two buildings," she said, with a shrug of her shoulders.

"Did your husband mention any stipulation about the developer buying both buildings?"

"No, he didn't mention anything like that."

"Did he mention whose idea it was?"

She looked puzzled for a second. "I don't recall discussing it with him specifically, but I got the impression that Dunne Development approached him."

"I understand you own this building. How do you feel about selling it?"

One of her employees walked in the door, interrupting before she could answer.

"Excuse me, Novie, there seems to be a problem with the soda order. What's being delivered isn't what was ordered, and Mike wants you to talk to the delivery guy." Novie shook her head in resignation, "They never get that order right; tell Mike I'll be there in a few minutes."

"I'm sorry, Mr. Hunter. What did you ask me?"

"I asked how you felt about selling this building."

"I inherited this building from my parents and when my husband first mentioned it, I was against it. A few years ago, no one was interested in opening a business here. All the department stores moved to the Mall while others went out of business. In some cases, the owners died and family members weren't interested in keeping the businesses going. There were just a few die-hard businesses that hung on: the lamp store down the street, the fruit-shipping store, and a few others. After my parents passed away, I decided this was my opportunity to fulfill my dream and theirs. It was a slow start but business has really boomed during the last three years. Anyway, my husband Rupert explained that I could still rent the space and keep the Ocean Street Café since the developer was not going to make any changes to the first floor; I told him I'd consider it. I know he wants me to sell, but I'm still thinking about it. Can you wait a few minutes while I take care of this soda problem?"

He looked at his watch for confirmation. "Actually, I have what I need for the time being, and I do have another appointment." He reached out to shake her hand. "Thank you for taking the time to talk to me." He gave her his business card and told her he'd be in touch.

"As anyone who has ever been around a cat for any length of time well knows cats have enormous patience with the limitations of the human kind."—Cleveland Amory

CHAPTER TWENTY-THREE: *The Opportune Time to Act*

I took a shortcut home and when I rounded the corner, I saw David Hunter's car parked in the convenience store's parking lot. The clerk inside the store barely glanced at the customers as she rang up their purchases, took their money, and made change. Naturally, I wanted to know why Hunter was sitting in his car, watching the clerk so intently. Hunter waited until the customers had all cleared out before he went in. I followed right behind him, unnoticed. I barely escaped having my tail clipped as the door shut automatically behind me.

Hunter asked the clerk if she was Sally Wakowycz, introduced himself, and told her why he was there. Sally was willing to answer his questions but didn't remember seeing Ethan that particular Saturday morning. She told him if it had been busy, she probably wouldn't have noticed him because as she got older she had to concentrate harder on what she was doing. This last statement was said *sotto voce* as she looked around to make sure no one else was within hearing range.

"I'm sorry I wasn't much help to you. I do remember Ethan—a handsome young man, and always polite. He may have been in the store on that particular day, and I just don't remember seeing him."

Hunter thanked her for her time, gave her his card, picked up a pack of gum, and paid for it with a five-dollar bill. He pocketed the change, and glanced at the receipt before dropping it in the trash can by the door.

She called out to him as he was halfway out the door, "How about the sales receipt? It has a date and time on it. Would that help?"

"Only if we can find it."

I scooted out of the automatic door which was closing slowly—again behind Hunter—being careful not to let him see me. I took off at a gallop before he left the parking lot, and arrived home at the same time as Maggie, barely making it through the front door before she did. I don't know how long it was before I heard the doorbell. Maggie let Hunter in, making the usual small talk as she led him to the kitchen.

"Did you have any trouble finding the house?"

"No, not at all. I was early and took a short drive around the residential area. I didn't realize how much has undergone redevelopment. This is a very attractive neighborhood."

"The redevelopment only extends a couple of miles around downtown, but I'm sure as more people rediscover the charm of these old houses, it will spread out."

"I see why you were being offered more than double what you paid for your property. The area definitely has potential," he remarked.

"I agree, and I realize it seems foolish of me to even consider selling our building, but we could have bought or rented somewhere else and made a nice profit."

Maggie pulled out a chair and sat down at the kitchen table, inviting him to do the same. Uninvited, I jumped up and sat on the chair next to Hunter, watching every move the lawyer made.

"I spoke with Ethan and he told me that he stopped at the convenience store around the corner to buy cat treats before you arrived." Hunter interrupted himself, looked directly at me, and asked Maggie if I was an indoor or an outdoor cat.

"Oh, they're strictly indoor cats. Why do you ask?"

"I thought I saw him or another cat that looks just like him around town." The lawyer scowled and gave me a puzzled look.

"Well, Murfy is full of surprises and you never know what he's up to, but I don't think it was him."

Hunter didn't look convinced.

"Getting back to what I was saying. The prosecutor, Everett Bixby has a witness who says he saw an SUV in your driveway ten minutes earlier than the time Ethan told the police he arrived. Ethan explained that he often brought cat treats and half-way up the driveway he realized he'd forgotten to buy any so he backed up and drove to the convenience store around the corner."

"That's true," said Maggie. "Whenever he forgets, Misty doesn't leave him alone, pawing at his pockets looking for her treat."

"Ethan stated that he had the bag in his hands when he walked in the house and put it on the counter. In your statement, you said you were right behind him. Did you see him with a bag?"

"I'm sorry; I don't remember one way or the other. No, wait. I did see the cat treats there," Maggie said, pointing to the counter next to the stove. "One day when I was here to feed the cats, I noticed one of the cats was missing, and I grabbed the treats from the bag to entice her back into the house."

"Did you see a receipt anywhere?"

"No, I don't think so."

"Is there anything left of the treats?"

"No, the cats didn't like them, so I threw them in the trash. Why?"

"At the very least, it proves that Ethan didn't lie about going to the convenience store."

Maggie's face was crestfallen. "I didn't know or I wouldn't have tossed them."

"Not your fault," said Hunter. "You had no way of knowing. Not much we can do about it now."

She gave him a weak smile.

"Alyx said the pot she was hit with was right up here on the end," Hunter stated as he stood up. "I always considered the space between cabinets and the ceiling wasted space, but I see Alyx made good use of it."

He was referring to the baskets of different sizes and shapes, some with silk plants spilling out; several copper items, and three pieces of pottery—all made by Ethan—that lined the highest reaches of the kitchen. He reached for the copper bowl next to where the pot had been. At six feet one, Hunter was one inch shorter than Ethan, and had no problem bringing it down.

I had been sizing up the lawyer as I listened to the discussion and sensed his ambivalent feelings towards cats. I didn't know exactly what lawyers did, but I knew this one was defending Ethan, doing the same thing I was—putting clues together to solve a puzzle.

I quickly determined that this was the opportune time to act. Although my theory as to what had happened remained unconfirmed, I wanted to get the lawyer thinking in that direction. I jumped off the chair and onto the counter, startling Hunter into reaching out for me, foiling my attempt to leap to the top of the cabinet.

Maggie literally snatched me out of his hands and unceremoniously deposited me on the floor. Naturally, I was mad and showed it by stomping out of the kitchen, definitely peeved, but I stayed close enough to hear the rest of the conversation.

"I don't know why he did that; he's usually very well behaved. I'm sorry I grabbed him out of your hands like that, but that hissing was so out of character, I was afraid he might bite you."

"I probably frightened him by reaching for him the way I did."

Hunter said he had what he needed, and Maggie walked him to the door.

"Thank you for taking the time to meet me here."

"Alyx and Ethan are the family I never had. If it weren't for Alyx, I wouldn't be living my dream now. When I met her, I was going to school full time and working full time. It was harder than I had imagined and I wanted to quit many times, but she wouldn't let me. She encouraged and sometimes browbeat me to continue. Had I not met Alyx, I would probably still be behind a cosmetics counter, waiting for the right man to come along. So please call me if there's anything I can do, anything at all."

"I will certainly do that."

"If you play with a cat, you must not mind her scratch."
—Anonymous

CHAPTER TWENTY-FOUR: *Elation and Disappointment*

I paced around the house thinking. Hunter had said that on the day Alyx was injured, Ethan came in carrying a small bag from the convenience store and set it down on the counter in the kitchen. Ethan must have taken the treats out of the bag Sunday evening—which was when he gave us the treats. Misty, who diligently keeps track of everyone, surely remembers him doing that. I confronted her.

Misty, fastidious about her grooming, was licking her paws. She immediately let me know I was intruding. She wanted to know why it was so important for Pooky to come in now that Alyx was conscious.

Distracted, I lost my patience. Hadn't she been paying attention? Didn't she hear the lawyer David Hunter talking about a receipt?

She was busy scratching behind her left ear, and she jumped straight up in the air when I pounced in front of her and asked about the receipt. She proudly announced that she did remember seeing something float to the floor when Ethan took the treats out of the bag.

I stayed outwardly calm while she tried to remember where Ethan was standing when he took the treats out of the bag. She walked around and stopped to the right of the stove. The way I figured it, the receipt must have floated under the stove, unless it didn't and the cleaning lady that Maggie had temporarily hired trashed it. The thought froze me to the spot, but only for a moment. I fell on my side and peered under the stove, excited when I saw the receipt. I stretched as far as I could, but it was still out of my reach.

Disappointed and discouraged, I stayed where I was, wondering how in the world I was going to communicate what I knew. Judging from the fiasco that had occurred with the lawyer earlier, it was doubtful.

"If man could be crossed with the cat, it would improve man, but it would deteriorate the cat."—Mark Twain

CHAPTER TWENTY-FIVE: *A Shopping Trip Remembered*

I worried about Alyx, and I visited as often as possible, and so far, I'd missed detection. I was there early Wednesday morning when the nurse checking her vital signs woke her up.

"How are you feeling this morning?"

"I feel fine, but I'm a little hungry."

"Sorry, breakfast won't be served for a while; let me see if I can find something for you." Sara, the nurse, smiled and said she would be right back.

On my previous visits, I had observed that Alyx did her best to be a model patient, cooperating with the staff, doing what they said without argument and had earned a good reputation among the staff.

Although everyone was kind to her, Nurse Sara Jones, a pleasant-looking woman about ten years older than Alyx, was especially so. Sara told her that having raised two children on her own, she understood a mother's emotional investment in her children. She told Alyx that she knew Ethan had been charged with attempted murder and she could imagine just how she'd feel if that had been one of her children in jail—guilty or not. Sara was back a few minutes later with a glass of orange juice and a package of saltine crackers. Seeing the crackers must have reminded Alyx of something. She immediately called David Hunter and left a message that she needed to speak to him as soon as possible.

A short time later that morning, Hunter's assistant, Dorinda, returned her call to let her know that Hunter had her message and that he would be in to see her before nine. In the meantime, Alyx flipped through all the reading material that Maggie had brought for her but not even her favorite mystery writer's new book could hold her interest for more than a few minutes. She put the book down and looked up expectantly when she heard someone come in.

"Dr. Casey will be in to talk to you when he makes his rounds later today, but I thought you'd be happy to know, he's going to let you go home tomorrow," Sara announced cheerfully.

"You don't know how happy I am to hear that."

"Yes, I do, sweetie," Sara said fluffing up her pillow. "I'm going home soon and I won't be on duty for the next two days. I just want to wish you and your son the best. I hope things work out for him. I've seen him at your side; I've heard him talking to you, and I don't believe he's guilty."

"Thank you for that, and for everything. When all this is over, Sara, please stop by Antiques & Designs and I'll treat you to coffee and the best homemade muffins in the city from the Ocean Street Café."

"You can count on it, if you'll make the coffee, green tea."

"You got it!"

Later, after she was back from her mid-morning stroll down the hospital corridors, Alyx had just slipped under the covers when David Hunter finally walked in. I, of course, was at my guard position behind the screen. Alyx visually relaxed when Hunter entered the hospital room. I don't know what that was all about, but whatever it was, she was glad to see him.

"Good morning, Alyx. How are you?"

"I feel fine now that the headaches have lessened. I've been allowed to walk around and I just learned I'll be released tomorrow."

"I'm glad to hear that." He took a small notebook from his briefcase, and pulled up a chair next to her.

"Thank you for coming so quickly. I was anxious to tell you about my purse being stolen recently."

"Actually," said Hunter, "Ethan told me about it and I had planned on coming to see you anyway. He said someone took your purse from your shopping cart at the grocery store and returned it within the hour with nothing missing. No one saw who took it or who returned it. Do you have anything to add to that?"

"It happened on a Saturday about three weeks ago; I don't know the date...as Ethan said, my purse was stolen from my grocery cart and returned within the hour, with nothing missing—not even the bills I had in the wallet. I thought it strange that someone would steal it and then return it with money and credit cards still there."

Hunter agreed.

"I don't usually put my purse in the cart while shopping, but the wheat crackers I wanted were on the top shelf and out of my reach. I put my purse in the cart so I could balance myself better as I stepped on the bottom shelf and reached up. When I put the box in the cart, I noticed my purse was gone."

"Did you see anyone walking away?"

"Yes; there were several people pushing their carts down the aisle; but no, I didn't see anyone carrying my purse or anyone who looked suspicious. That's pretty much it, except, it was obvious someone had looked at everything in my purse, especially my wallet. I found things in different places than they had been."

"What kind of information did they have access to?"

"Literally, my life!"

David raised a questioning eyebrow, "How do you mean?"

"My driver's license, credit cards, debit, and ATM cards were in my purse. My checkbook was in it, as well as my house and car keys. Because my business cards were also in my purse, they would know about that part of my life too."

"What did you do to protect yourself from identity theft?"

"I reported the theft to the police and made calls to have my accounts closed and new cards issued. I called Ethan to bring a spare set of keys and asked him to replace the lock on the front door."

"Did he change the lock?"

"No; I told him not to bother, because right after I got home, the grocery store called to tell me that someone had found my purse. Since whoever took it, returned it within the hour with nothing missing I didn't think it was necessary."

"Did the store get the name of the person who turned it in?"

"The store manager said it just appeared on the Customer Service counter; the clerk behind the counter didn't see anyone put it down."

"Whoever took your purse could have had another key made during that hour that it was missing."

"At the time, I thought whoever took it had a change of heart and decided to return it."

"And now?"

"Now I'm not sure. You think someone had a key made and tried to rob me Saturday morning?"

"That may have been the original intent of the thief, but it seems unlikely that he/they would have tried to rob you in broad daylight, key or no key…I'm going to look further into this, and I'll call you if I need any more information. In the meantime, I strongly suggest you have the lock changed immediately, before you go home, in fact."

"I like to believe the best of people, but I know there are criminals out there. I'll ask Maggie to take care of that."

"Good." He reviewed his notes once more. "There is just one more thing that needs clearing up. Do you remember specifically locking both locks on your door when you retrieved your paper Saturday morning?"

She bit her lower lip, deep in concentration. "I don't remember. I'm in the habit of always locking the door when I'm home, but I don't remember specifically if I locked either lock, or any for that matter. I'm sorry."

It sounded like David Hunter was out of questions. He put his notebook away, and stood to leave. "I'm meeting with a private investigator I use for tough cases, and I'll have him look into this also. I'll be in my office for the next couple of hours if you have anything else."

"If cats could talk, they wouldn't."—Nan Porter

CHAPTER TWENTY-SIX: *Star Witness Returns*

Thursday, five days after Pooky disappeared, low clouds grounded the flight school students at the nearby airport, making it a quiet day over Beachside. Mindful of the fact that no one can force a cat to do anything he doesn't want to do; I simply had to wait for Pooky to make the decision to come in. The way I figured it, she was probably ready to do that anytime now.

Misty had the watch, and she confessed as soon as it happened that she had dozed off and missed Pooky's return. She said the rain made her tired and she closed her eyes for just a minute, and when she opened them, she saw a flash of black fur sliding out of the screened porch.

I was disappointed, but my comment was positive. "It's good that she showed herself. Maybe if it keeps raining she'll call it quits."

As I predicted, later that morning, a bedraggled Pooky slid through the partially-open screen door. I motioned to Misty to slip away as we had previously discussed. Pooky looked a little thinner and dirtier, but okay otherwise. I watched unobtrusively from inside as she hungrily ate—pausing to look around before she took a drink. Familiar with the handicap, I knew how hard it must have been for her to catch anything to eat outdoors without claws.

I lay on my side, facing her, my non-aggressive stance signaling that I wouldn't harm her. When it appeared that she was finished, I slowly got up, slipped through the cat door, kept a comfortable distance between us, and allowed her time to rest. Out of the corner of my eye, I saw Misty edging closer and I gave her a look. A slash of my tail confirmed I was serious. Misty moved away, but not too far.

I stayed crouched by the cat door, and kept my eyes on both Pooky and Misty. As soon as Pooky woke up, Misty rushed out. Believing she was under attack, Pooky followed her natural instincts and ran. I charged after her.

With no destination in mind, Pooky zigzagged across the yard, slithering under bushes and around trees, until she suddenly stopped. A raccoon—bigger and heavier than us—slowly traversed the yard just a few feet away, maybe on his way to or back from searching garbage cans, or pets' food bowls left outside.

For a few tense moments, we stared at one another trying to gage the degree of threat each presented. With razor sharp claws on human-like hands, raccoons are vicious fighters who do attack pets. I didn't see any reason to prove that point. I backed up slowly and recommended Pooky do the same, allowing the raccoon to pass through. She trotted back to the house, and I followed at a quick pace, frequently looking over my shoulder, ready to stand and fight, if necessary. Apparently, the raccoon didn't intend to detour from his course and continued on his path.

It was much later, after everyone had calmed down, that I found out what had happened on Saturday morning before Pooky ran away.

Her story was that she was relaxing on the floor behind my chair when a lizard crossed in front of her. She was bored and thought it would be fun to chase it around for a bit. She was right behind it as it scuttled into the kitchen. Alyx was sitting at the kitchen table with her back to the dining room doorway—she may have heard Pooky, but she didn't see her. I asked Pooky to demonstrate what she did and ushered the girls into the kitchen.

Pooky looked up to where the pot had been. She demonstrated that she had jumped up on the counter and leaped to the top of the wall cabinet, lost her balance, and knocked the pot down. Then, she had run back into the dining room, hid under the hutch and stayed there until she had the opportunity to run out.

As far as I was concerned, what had happened was an accident. I still didn't understand why Pooky had run away. She explained that when her former humans first brought her home with them as a kitten, they were very understanding of cat behaviors, but as she got older, they became more intolerant. They became very angry when she scratched their brand-new coffee table and ruined their sheer drapes. She knew they didn't want her climbing on things, but she couldn't help it and a few of their items got broken.

At that point, she seemed unsure if she should continue, and I encouraged her to go on; I wanted to hear the rest of the story.

She thought her former owners were playing a game with her when they let her out of the car. She thought they wanted her to play in the tall grass, but the car left just as she bounded away. She ran back to the spot where her humans had left her and waited for them to come back for her. They never did.

That first day out in the unfamiliar setting was very scary and unsettling for a young cat that had only known a cage at an animal shelter, and then a comfortable home. Pooky had no idea where she was or what she should do. Tired and hungry, she moved away from the road and found a sheltered spot under a palmetto bush. She couldn't stop trembling as she tried to remember some key points about being outdoors and hunting for food, but there wasn't much to remember. Separated from her mother at a very young age, she had not received any of the training a cat usually gets from its mother. All she knew about hunting was what she had heard from some of the cats she had lived with before her adoption.

She fondly remembered one sage tiger cat talking about what it was like living outdoors. He had belonged to a colony of feral cats. That was the only way of life he knew and he missed it terribly. The tiger cat liked to re-live the good times by telling the younger cats about his hunting expeditions, making it sound easy and fun. Pooky decided while she was out there in the open, that she would try some of the tactics that Mr. Tiger had told them about the next morning. In the meantime, she would stay put—maybe by then the trembling would stop. Morning came and went and she still had not moved. When her body was finally still, the hunger pangs stirred her to explore the area. As she skulked about, she munched on leaves of plants that looked okay to eat, although she didn't know much about that either. She hoped she wouldn't eat anything that made her sick—or worse—poison her.

She haltingly moved through the vegetation, hiding every time she heard an unfamiliar sound. Her long luxurious fur started tangling, and eventually pulled out as she slid through dead branches and thick bushes.

She did catch a few insects—one baby lizard during the day—but by evening, her stomach was growling, and her mouth was dry. She heard some chirping up ahead, and silently approaching, she saw three small birds feeding on the ground. She tried the hide-wait-pounce method Mr. Tiger had described, but it didn't work; the birds flew out of reach.

And so it went for the rest of the night and the following day as she trekked through what she thought was a never-ending jungle, but knew from the sounds and smells that she was not far from human habitats.

She looked around for a sheltered place to rest and found a hole created by a pile of debris, supported by two large branches. Some mice were exploring the area nearby and this time her hide-wait-pounce method netted her a baby mouse for dinner, and on her meandering walk back to the hideout, she found a ditch that still had a trickle of water left from the rain earlier in the week which allowed her to quench her thirst.

Full for the first time in days, she began to think that maybe she would be okay after all. Safe in her hideout, she thought how nice it would be if she could find a clowder to join as Mr. Tiger had found.

The lively meowing in the distance tempted her to cautiously venture out of her hideout. She approached quietly and kept out of sight, observing the small group of cats. They didn't look as well kept or well fed as Mr. Tiger had led her to believe outdoor cats would look like. They didn't look any better than she did—and she knew she looked awful. As soon as the feral colony became aware of her presence, the cats tensed and the biggest of the group—a tortoise male—stepped forward and turned in her direction. Apparently, Mr. Tiger had forgotten to mention that feral cats didn't accept stray cats into their colonies.

Pooky slowly backed up, her heart beating in her ears, and when a safe distance away, ran as fast as her weakened body would let her until she was safe back in her hole. She curled her body tight, and buried her face in her paws, blotting out the harsh reality.

Things didn't get any better over the next two weeks. She had trouble catching anything as her clawless paws made it almost impossible for her to hold on to anything but the smallest mammals. The insects and vegetation she ate weren't enough to sustain her and the water supply was gone. She became weaker and weaker to the point where even the parasites she had acquired, left her body, because there was less and less for them to feed on. She kept losing weight and was literally skin and bones.

Eventually, she did find some kind humans who gave her food and water when she appeared at their door but not enough to sustain her ravaged body and by the time she found Alyx, she was dying. She knew she owed Alyx her life and was profoundly sorry for what had happened.

Saturday, when she heard the pot break, she feared that Alyx would want to get rid of her and bring her to one of those *humane* places that no one ever wants to talk about, even if someone does make it out alive. When she heard that Alyx was hurt, she thought she might have a better chance outdoors on her own.

I let her know that it didn't bother me so much what she thought of Misty and me, but she should have known better than to think Alyx would get rid of her because of the accident; she wasn't like that.

Pooky lowered her head, and apologized again. Pooky said she couldn't let Ethan be locked up for something he didn't do, and insisted that she wanted to do something to make up for the problems she had caused. She was sincere, and I sincerely needed help; I couldn't be in two places at once and some places not at all.

Pooky said she could help with that. While living on the street, she'd made some friends in the neighborhood. She suggested that since the weather was so nice, most windows would be open and it would be no problem for a cat to hear a conversation going on inside.

I kept pacing, frustrated to have solved the case and not be able to free Ethan. In reality, what human was going to take me seriously? As Pooky stated, humans have limited imagination and since I couldn't read, write, or talk, I was just a cat who looked and behaved like any other cat. Chances were that the expensive lawyer David Hunter would keep doing what he did, spinning his wheels and coming up with nothing. Hunter had said that putting Alyx on the stand was Ethan's best chance, even though she hadn't seen who had hit her. He said her testimony would weigh heavily with the jury, but would it be enough to keep Ethan from serving jail time?

I had no choice. I had to show Alyx what had happened, even if it might make me look guilty—which the girls were quick to point out.

There was an audible silence while I paced, thinking that I had to know what Hunter had uncovered so I would know what to do next—what information to communicate, to whom and how, and most important, I needed to know if there was anything immediate going on that threatened Alyx or Ethan's safety.

I told Pooky I welcomed anything she could do to help.

"I have studied many philosophers and many cats. The wisdom of cats is infinitely superior."—Hippolyte Taine

CHAPTER TWENTY-SEVEN: *The Defense Stumbles*

David Hunter lived in another city but his office was on the peninsula right across the old Broadway Bridge, currently closed to traffic. Pooky was right about open windows in good weather. One particular window in Hunter's office was low enough for me to see inside if I stood on my hind legs, and the shrubs up against the foundation were large enough to hide me.

The well-appointed, large corner office had plenty of light from the two windows in the room. The plush carpet was a dark shade of green. A mahogany desk faced the door, with two green leather armchairs in front of it, the low credenza for the coffeemaker and coffee mugs behind the desk. A brown leather couch sat against one wall. Bookshelves filled with law books lined the rest of the wall space. The total effect was one of order and success.

Hunter arrived soon after I had positioned myself on the window sill, with a man—lean and muscular with eyes so dark they were almost black. He was handsome, in a rough sort of way, or at least Hunter's assistant thought so judging from the way she was acting. The scar over his left eye, enhanced, rather than detracted from his good looks.

He stopped at her desk for a moment. "Hi, Dorinda, nice to see you again."

She smiled at him in a peculiar way. "Hi, Tim, it's nice to see you too. I'm still waiting for you to tell me how you got that scar. Will you ever tell me?" Dorinda wanted to know.

He winked at her, "Maybe one day I'll tell you."

Hunter, waiting in the doorway to his office, rolled his eyes and groaned. "Will you stop flirting with my assistant and come in my office?"

"So what's up?" the man asked. "Am I here to discuss the case as a professional or as the only friend you have?"

"Both. I want your professional opinion and possibly your help, and I want you to remind me what a great lawyer I am because, frankly, I'm baffled."

Hunter pulled a file out and set it on the desk in front of him. My guess was that the file was Ethan's. "Take a look at this and tell me what I'm missing."

Tim poured himself a cup of coffee, and sat down to review the file while Hunter stepped out to the outer office.

When he walked back in, Tim was refilling his cup. "What about Alyx's ex-husband? I don't see anything on him."

David sat behind his desk and leaned back. Tim sat facing him, legs stretched out in front, his fingers laced in a steeple.

"The ex is the one who hired me; I speak to him often. Nothing there. They only occasionally communicate and, more important, there's no motive. My understanding is that they're not the best of friends, but they don't hate each other either."

Tim raised a questioning eyebrow. "I didn't see any transcribed interview for Ethan here in the file. What did he have to say?"

"It hasn't been typed yet. I have it right here."

Hunter clicked the play button and skipped it forward. Hunter's voice and Ethan's responses poured forth from the machine:

"Your father overheard Maggie talking to someone about moving the store to another location. Did she discuss it with you?"

"Yeah, Maggie called me about it last Thursday. She said a real estate broker contacted her and told her the developer of the condominiums going up down the street was interested in buying their property, offering double what they had originally paid. Maggie thought it was worth thinking about, but Mom just got mad at her. Maggie wanted me to bring it up again to Mom just to explain that Maggie didn't necessarily want to sell but that the offer should be discussed."

"How do you feel about selling?"

"Me? I don't have any say in that."

"Well, you're part owner with your mother, aren't you?"

"Yeah, I guess, but that's only on paper. I'm not involved in any decision making—and I don't want to be."

"Did you talk to your mother about it?"

"No, I didn't get the chance. I was going to bring it up at breakfast on Saturday, but I didn't know Maggie was going to be there too, so I probably wouldn't have said anything about it."

Pause.

"I know why you're asking me," Ethan continued. "I swear the only reason I agreed with Maggie to bring it up to Mom was that I didn't want anything to break up their friendship or partnership; I've never seen Mom happier and I would never do anything to change that."

"Okay; I know we've been over this, but sometimes small details that seem unimportant are left out. Tell me again what happened Saturday morning. Start from the beginning—from the time you left your building and don't leave anything out, no matter how small or insignificant you think it is."

"You want to know if I spoke to someone in the parking lot?"

"Yes, who you spoke to, who you saw, what you saw and what you heard."

"Yea, right. I don't usually get up before noon on weekends, and I was reluctant to get up to have breakfast with Mom at ten. I took a shower, didn't shave—didn't have time to shape the black stubble on my face, soon to be a chinstrap beard.

I left my apartment, going down the outside stairs, taking the steps two at a time. I almost ran into a beautiful girl about my age—tall and slender, with short blond hair and slanted blue eyes, or maybe turquoise. I don't know. The color is hard to describe. I introduced myself and she said her name was Nikki.

She was lost and asked me for directions, which I gave her. She was looking for the guy who lives next door. You know how that goes; some guys have all the luck.

Before I climbed in my car, I saw this Nikki pause at the top of the stairs and look back. I smiled and waved. She waved back.

When I turned the key in the ignition, I noticed I was almost out of gas. I didn't have time to stop at my favorite station a couple of miles in the opposite direction, so I stopped, instead, at the one along the way where gas is usually a little higher. Standing there at the pump, watching the dollar amount race along made me think about the mess I had made of my finances even after all the warnings from Mom about spending.

After thinking about it, I decided to swallow my pride and ask Mom for help, telling myself how much worse it would be if I had to move back home because I couldn't afford to pay the rent.

I was sure that's what Mom wanted to discuss with me, and my stomach churned when I saw Maggie's car pull up the driveway. It's not that I don't like her; she's pretty cool. I just didn't think I could handle both of them ganging up on me.

I turned the knob on the door and took out my key when the door didn't open. While I waited for Maggie to get out of the car and come to the door, I could hear the cats' loud, distressed meowing. I had a feeling something was wrong, and I was sure of it when Mom didn't answer my greeting. I ran to the kitchen and saw her slumped forward on the table. I checked her pulse, pulled a towel from the drawer and pressed on the gash on her head. I told Maggie to call 911 and we waited for the ambulance. And that's it."

"According to my notes, the last time we spoke, you said you saw a blue car in front of your mother's house that drove away as you turned down her street. Was it parked there?"

"I don't know. All I saw was the brake lights flash briefly and the car driving away."

"Could you tell the make of the car?"

"Naw; I really wasn't paying close attention. For all I know, it could have just been going down the street and the driver hit the breaks for whatever reason."

"Did you see the driver?"

"No."

"You told Detective Smarts that you found the door locked and used your key to get in. Did you use your key to unlock both locks?"

"What difference does that make?"

"I understand your frustration; please bear with me. If the dead bolt was on, then the perpetrator would have had to have a key to lock it back up when he left, on the other hand, anyone could have turned the knob on the other lock from inside, locking the door behind them. That helps our case because it means anyone else could have entered, not just you."

"Yeah, I understand, but I don't know. The door didn't open when I turned the knob. I was distracted by the cats' loud meowing; I don't remember which one I unlocked."

"Okay, that's enough for today. I'm on my way to speak to Maggie next and hear what she has to say about the real estate proposal she received. Are you doing okay? Anything you want me to do?"

"I want you to get me out of here. There's this crazy tattooed man who killed another homeless man, stabbing him ten times because he touched his rusty old bicycle. He rambles on all day and all night... I'm about to go crazy myself. Please, get me out of here."

"That's what I'm trying to do, Ethan. I'll see you soon." With that, Hunter clicked off the recorder and glanced over at the man Tim. My ears perked up.

"I see you have a note here about Ethan seeing a blue car in front of his mother's house, and I heard you question him in the taped interview," said Tim, "but there's no follow up on it. Why?"

"I wasn't sure there was enough to pursue it after I interviewed Moresby," said Hunter. "That interview hasn't been typed yet either, you'll have to listen to it.

"There were only two cars in the parking lot of the small stand-alone building when I arrived," said Hunter, "a blue expensive foreign make, and a red economy one."

"I walked in and Rupert Moresby—easily recognized from his picture in the real estate ads which is a good thing in the real estate business—stood at the reception desk speaking to the young woman sitting there. I introduced myself, and Moresby, slightly stooped as if carrying a heavy load in his arms, with thinning, dirty blonde hair and a walrus mustache, offered a limp handshake. I assumed other realtors occupied the other three offices, but at that moment we were the only three people in the building.

"He made it very clear that he didn't know anything about what had happened to Alyx, and didn't understand why I was there asking questions.

"I asked him who was interested in the Antiques & Designs building, and he said that James Dunne, the developer who's putting up the condominiums down the street, was interested in buying it and the one next door. Dunne already owns the building next to the Ocean Street Café, and the one on the other side of Antiques & Designs. His plan is to add a third floor and convert the top two floors into condominiums, keeping the bottom floor as retail space. Paying six hundred thousand dollars for one building is a good deal for him when you consider that he'll be able to sell each unit for at least three to four hundred thousand dollars."

Tim agreed. "There's no question he would stand to make a sizeable profit. Was he aware that Alyx didn't want to sell?"

"Yes, Maggie had told him, and he admitted that he was upset at first."

"What about Dunne Development? What do you know about them?" prodded Tim.

"Dunne Development is a well-known and respected firm. I know James Dunne, the owner, and we've played golf for various charities. I called him right after I spoke with Moresby and chatted about the charity golf tournament coming up next month and business in general.

"I asked him about his involvement with Rupert Moresby. He said Moresby presented it as a straightforward business deal. He told Jim he could deliver the two buildings between the two that he already owned. At first, Jim thought it would only be feasible if he had both buildings but after thinking about it, he realized he could do it by just purchasing one of the buildings. It would cut into his profit, but still come out ahead and so would Moresby."

"When did he tell Rupert he could still proceed with just one of the buildings?" asked Tim.

"He didn't."

"Well… what can I do to help you my friend?"

"I was hoping you could help me out with the purse-snatchers," said Hunter. "It's a real long shot, I know, but you never know where it might lead. It's possible they tried to rob Alyx. If they're professionals, they probably wore gloves, and there wouldn't be any other fingerprints around the house or on the pot. And then again, if they're professionals, they wouldn't have tried to rob her in daylight."

"Right. And if they were watching her, they would have known her work schedule. She said Saturday is always her day off."

"And since they ignored all that, why didn't they take anything?"

"That's a good question, and I don't have an answer. Maybe Ethan and Maggie's arrival scared them away."

"That means that whoever attacked her meant to do just that."

Hunter lightly hit the corner of the desk with his fist. "I have successfully defended some who were no doubt guilty and here's an innocent young man who will probably have to serve time if I can't defend him against the evidence gathered by the State Attorney's Office."

Hunter rose from his chair and paced the length of the room. "A review of the scene revealed no sign of a break-in or struggle, nothing taken or disturbed. The only prints on the pot belong to Ethan and Alyx. The witness reports confirm that Ethan's car and Maggie's were the only cars seen in the driveway. The police learned that Alyx's half of the business was in both their names. The interview with Maggie also revealed Ethan's bout of depression over the break-up with his long-time girlfriend just four months earlier. The police also know that Alyx had expressed her concern over Ethan's spending habits, had quarreled with him on several occasions, most recently, about his twenty-five thousand dollar purchase of a Harley-Davidson motorcycle.

"The next-door neighbor, Mrs. Leary, told the police about the day Ethan showed up on his Harley. She was out on the porch, heard the motorcycle drive up, and the ensuing argument when Alyx came out, adding at the end, that it really sounded more like a disagreement than an argument. Unfortunately, that last part didn't make it into the report."

Tim leaned forward. "I see why you're concerned. It doesn't look good for the kid."

"Notwithstanding all that, Ethan refuses to plead guilty or make any deals; says he abhors even the thought of being associated with such a heinous crime, let alone plead guilty. He insists he's innocent—that he would rather take his chances. That hope is dashed now that she's regained consciousness and doesn't know who tried to kill her."

"She can testify in his defense, though, can't she?"

"She wants to. I haven't made a decision on that."

Both men were silent long enough for me to think they'd left the room, when Hunter came to stand in front of the window. I quickly moved out of his line of vision, pulling out some fur as I backed deeper in the thorny bushes.

Tim said, "I think we should talk to Mr. Moresby again. If it turns out that he was involved in the attack, it might prompt him to make a move. And what about this guy…George Lucas? You want me to talk to him?"

Hunter said, "I already have. I recorded the interview. I don't have any notes because he didn't have anything to add, but if you want to take it on, see if you can dig up anything on his business dealings, past and present."

"Okay; so I'm to look into both the purse-snatching and Mr. Moresby…and check George Lucas' business dealings. Right?"

"Right."

"How quickly do you want me to get on it?"

"Quick."

Their voices sounded farther away now and I took one quick look into the room.

Tim was looking at his phone. "I just happen to have some time in the next couple of days, is that quick enough?" Hunter sat behind his desk. Tim finished off the last of his coffee and got up to leave.

"Got to go. I have a lunch date in ten minutes and this lady doesn't cut me any slack," he said, grinning. How are things with you and Joann?"

"Still unsettled. Still a mess."

"I guess dinner with me and my lady is out of the question?"

"I'm afraid so," Hunter sighed audibly. "She filed the divorce papers; we've agreed to a settlement—she can't decide to let me go or hang on, but that's another story."

So there was a Mrs. Hunter, after all. I made my way home, dodging bikes, kids and dogs, devastated to hear Hunter admit that Ethan didn't have a chance. When I arrived home, I was exhausted, but I wasn't finished yet. I asked Pooky if she still wanted to help and she said she did. I asked her to arrange for one of her outdoor cat friends to stake out Hunter's office, on the lookout for Tim and report what he uncovered in his investigation.

"We have a theory that cats are planning to take over the world, just try to look them straight in the eye...yup, they're hiding something!"—Dog Fancy Magazine

CHAPTER TWENTY-EIGHT: *Dead-End Leads*

As promised, Hunter's friend Tim delivered the information two days later, and Pooky's friend was there to observe and report back to Pooky. Tim told Hunter that Moresby didn't want to talk at first. He told Tim that Hunter knew everything he knew and he had nothing else to say. Then, when Tim told Moresby that somebody had seen his car in front of Alyx's home, he became more talkative. He admitted to going to see her. He said that since he hadn't yet heard back from Maggie, he couldn't be sure that she had mentioned the deal to Alyx, so he decided to go speak to Alyx himself, but changed his mind when he got to Alyx's house and drove off without stopping. Hunter didn't think that was much to go on, but Tim thought it could motivate Moresby to make another move if he was involved.

Apparently, Tim had also spoken to the store manager regarding Alyx's purse snatching and the manager said that a long-time employee had dropped off the purse at the Customer Service counter. He spoke to the woman and she said she had found the purse on the floor, in the produce aisle on her way to the break-room. She said she didn't give an explanation to the Customer Service clerk because the girl was busy and she didn't want to use her break time waiting for her. She meant to tell her later but just forgot. The woman who had found the purse was seventy-years-old and had worked at that store for ten years in food demonstration.

According to Pooky's informant, Tim requested and received a copy of the video from the store's security office. The first time Tim and Hunter viewed the video, the surveillance camera panned the parking lot and store entrances and focused on the grocery store entrance. They saw Alyx enter the store with her purse, and leave empty-handed a short time later, but didn't see anyone suspicious or known to them. The two men viewed the video a second time and saw a man with a walrus mustache—Moresby's trademark—enter the coffee shop minutes after Alyx entered the grocery store. Since the coffee shop is part of the grocery store and the two places open to each other, Hunter said he would discuss it Moresby.

Tim said he had spoken to several sources and did some record-checking on George Lucas. It turned out that he had been sort of involved in a scandal a few years back. That is, Lucas wasn't personally involved, but the antique dealer he did business with was indicted for fraud and sentenced to prison. The police report said they were on an anonymous call, so George could have been the whistle blower on the case.

I commended Pooky's friend Jemma for a job well done. Pooky reported that Jemma said she liked being a snitch and had offered to stay on the case for as long as it took. I didn't particularly like the role I had been thrust into (that of inducing young felines into a life of espionage), but I was honor bound to do whatever needed to be done to keep my human safe.

"Cats are notoriously sore losers. Coming in second best,
especially to someone as poorly coordinated as a human being,
grates their sensibility."—Stephen Baker

CHAPTER TWENTY-NINE: *Attack Cats*

I panicked when Maggie walked in and found us all on the screened porch. It had cost Alyx a bundle to have the cat door installed on the glass patio door. She would be very upset if she found out it was for nothing. Fortunately, Maggie focused on Pooky and didn't seem to suspect anything, or didn't show it if she did.

"Well, my goodness, the prodigal cat has returned. I'm glad you decided to come home, Pooky. Alyx would have been really disappointed not to find you here."

"You must have had quite an adventure out there, but this better be the last of your outdoor excursions. The outside can be a very dangerous place for a kitty." She stood still for a second, her head cocked, and my heart stopped.

"How did you all get out here, anyway? I don't remember unlocking the cat door." She shook her head and gave Pooky another hug, brought her in and cleaned her up as much as Pooky would allow.

I felt intense relief when she didn't pay any attention to the screen door and left it propped open. I took a moment to catch my breath, and followed Maggie as she went about her established routine, one of which was to return calls to mutual friends, bringing them up to date on what was happening with Alyx and Ethan, while the other felines kept track of the activity in the back yard. After refilling the food and water bowls, Maggie went from room to room opening windows.

Her cell phone started playing the catchy tune Ethan had downloaded for her. It was Alyx calling, and I reached up with my paws, meowing and purring. She understood and hoisted me over her shoulder.

"Murfy wants to say hello; here he is," she said putting the phone to my ear. I heard Alyx talking and pretended nonchalance as expected. Maggie pressed the phone to her ear then, and Alyx said the doctor usually made his rounds at eight o'clock in the morning, and she would call after that to let her know what time to pick her up. Elated to hear that Alyx was coming home, I launched myself out of Maggie's arms and skidded across the tile floor to let the girls in on the good news.

The morning light squeezing through the partially closed shutters revealed the party atmosphere of the previous night: toys scattered all over, pillows knocked on the floor, and scatter rugs scattered. Too excited to sleep during the night, we had chased each other and a lizard all over the house. The lizard had lost his tail as a result. Lucky for him, we were too happy to take the hunt seriously.

I thought the girls could help with putting their toys back in the basket, work together to straighten the kitchen rugs, and put the pillows back on the couch. The tail, however, had to be disposed of immediately. For some reason not quite clear to me, humans reacted very badly to finding animal parts in a house. Alyx's shriek the first time I brought her a piece of lizard—was not soon forgotten. I picked up the tail with my teeth and dropped it in the wastebasket under the kitchen sink, the cabinet doors no problem.

I always hoped Alyx would toss bits of food into the garbage can, but she almost always disposed of any leftovers in the noisy contraption visible under the sink. By the time Maggie arrived, there was no sign of the previous night's celebration.

Maggie had arranged to have the front door lock re-keyed and the young man from All-Locks finished the job around ten. Maggie handed him a check and accepted the two keys he offered. I followed her as she closed and locked the windows. The phone rang before she got to Alyx's bedroom and I heard the one-sided conversation.

"Of course, I'll be there. I'm at your house now. Anything special you want me to bring you tomorrow morning?"

Maggie gathered Alyx's clothes; put them in a canvas tote bag and left. I divided my time between catnaps, and watching the street in hopes that Alyx might come home that day. Every time I heard a car in the distance, I sat tall in anticipation only to be disappointed when it wasn't Maggie.

That evening, I saw the same vehicle I had seen twice during the day slow down as it passed the house. I didn't recognize the driver or his passenger and warning bells went off in my head.

Sometime late into the night, a loud yowling outside rudely awakened me. The bully I had fought earlier that week had been taunting me since. I was sorry I hadn't hurt him more than I did when I had the chance.

I meandered to the front door and sat watching the scruffy stray, thinking I should go out there and force him out of the yard once-and-for-all, when the cat bounded away as fast as he could. I had no idea what had made the cat run away. I didn't think it was another animal or human because I hadn't heard any other sound. I stepped away from the glass, hid a little behind the door and continued to watch with interest.

There was no direct light illuminating the front porch, just the streetlight filtering through the branches of the large magnolia tree. Two men dressed in dark clothing, wearing dark wool caps approached from behind the azalea bushes.

The men were both at the front door; one of them crouched next to the wicker chair, the other one apparently trying a key in the lock. I couldn't believe what was happening and came out in full view as the man unsuccessfully tried to unlock the door. The man swore quietly as he motioned to his partner to check the windows. Misty and Pooky joined me growling and hissing at the intruders as we ran from window to window. Misty wasn't sure what was going on but she didn't let that stop her.

At Alyx's bedroom window, emboldened by the fact they were now in the dark and out of view from the street, the two men removed the screen. We were ready for them, a determined mass of fur, claws, and teeth.

In the melee, we scratched, bit, yowled, and squawked loud enough to wake up Smooch, the dog next door, who in turn woke up Mrs. Leary, who turned on her patio lights. The bloodied intruders ran off to the other side of the yard and down the street.

There wasn't anything I could do about the open window, but I reassured everyone not to worry about those two coming back. Proud of successfully defending our turf, the females rehashed everything that happened several times. Huddled on Alyx's bed, they finally fell into a light sleep and I watched the window through slit eyes, alert to the slightest sound.

"After dark all cats are leopards."—Native American Proverb

CHAPTER THIRTY: *Suspicion Falls On the Cats*

Alyx was finally home! "Hi, kitty-cats," she said, picking up and hugging each of us in turn and we did what cats do—rubbed against her ankles, purring and chattering all at the same time. "I've missed you too, fur-babies."

I hoped our jubilation welcoming her home wasn't more than what she needed. She looked pale, had lost a little weight and her clothes were loose on her. She sat on the couch and we surrounded her, leaving just enough room for Maggie to sit.

"Maggie, I'm sorry I snapped at you this morning."

Maggie smiled. "You did look funny sitting there in your hospital gown, ready to go, clothes or no clothes."

"Well, you said we had a ten o'clock appointment to visit Ethan and I was anxious."

"You told me to come at nine and I was early," Maggie answered. "Visitors are required to check in ten minutes before their appointment and we had plenty of time."

The stressful events had taken their toll on the friends. The friendship was strong, but not immune to the stresses inflicted on it by the recent events.

Alyx caught the defensive tone of the statement and hugged her quickly. "Yes, you were early, and I was anxious beyond reason."

"That was evident by the way you sat rigid in the passenger seat, looking out the window, hands clasped tight on your lap."

"A wave of emotions rolled over me as we pulled in the parking lot of that huge facility. I wasn't expecting the terror that settled around my heart as I looked at the multitude of men behind the tall, razor-wire fences. I understand that Ethan is just another victim of the imperfect laws of men, and I guess the majority of those people belong there but there must be others like Ethan who don't."

"That's true according to the news stories we often hear about men who have been falsely imprisoned."

"I know there has to be law and order, and punishment for those who break the law, but seeing men caged like animals is degrading to the human race. On the other hand, I realize the crimes some of those men have committed disqualify them as humans."

"You believe in the death penalty, then?" asked Maggie.

"That's a tough question to answer. At one time, I did, without a doubt. Now, I'm not sure. I think you've already taken someone's life when you lock him up. Once a person loses his freedom, what's there to live for? And the possibility of killing an innocent man is appalling. It gives me the shivers thinking about Ethan among murderers, rapists, pedophiles..."

"Like you, at one time I had no doubt it was the right thing to do. Some argue that even the Bible condones it. Now, I just don't know. Sometimes, when I hear of the crimes that have been committed, death seems too easy a punishment. I want them to suffer like they made their victims suffer."

The two women were silent for a moment, then Maggie said, "I'm glad that's not a decision I have to make. Anyway, tell me what happened after I dropped you off."

"The guard behind the desk, a hard young man who lost his battle with acne, directed me to the visitation room and searched me. It made me nervous when the door closed behind me in a long, narrow room with video screens along the two long walls. I looked forward to seeing Ethan and dreaded it at the same time. The room was full. There were two chairs and two phones in front of the screens—the areas separated by short walls. Ethan was already there, on the screen. He smiled and his face brightened when I picked up the phone, but I had already seen the pale withdrawn look on his face, in my eyes, the face of a sad and frightened little boy.

My heart was breaking as I tried my best to sound optimistic about the future. Knowing him as well as I do, I knew he was trying to do the same for my sake; the weariness reflected in his eyes told a different story. Neither of us brought up the actual subject of attempted murder until the thirty-minute visit was almost up. He said not to worry, that he could take care of himself. I hope he can. I'm not sure if self-confidence is a good thing or not in this case. One good thing is that he has confidence in his lawyer, and I know it makes a world of difference to have his father involved."

Alyx looked tired. Maggie suggested she go to bed and she didn't argue. I followed her quietly to her room. There, she saw all the items that had been on the chest were now on the floor, the window open and the screen on the ground. She closed the window, and put everything back on the chest, changed into pajamas and lay across the bed waiting for Maggie to bring her things from the hospital.

"Can I get you anything before I leave?" Maggie asked when she entered the room.

"No, I'm fine," she replied, pointing to the window, "but I'm wondering if you opened the window in here, by chance?"

"Yes, I did. Yesterday was such a beautiful day, I thought the house could stand some fresh air and I opened all the windows," she answered, looking at the closed window. "Why?"

"It's no big deal, but the window was open and the screen is outside on the ground. I was hoping it was you who forgot to close it rather than someone trying to get in."

"Oh, Alyx, I'm sorry. I feel terrible about this. I was in the process of closing the windows when you called me yesterday and I guess I just forgot to come back to this one."

"It's okay; don't worry about it. I will feel better, though, if you check the rest of the house, just in case."

She did, and they were all secure.

Maggie hadn't left yet when the doorbell rang. I trailed after Maggie to the front door. The police officer there asked to speak to Alyx.

"I just brought her home from the hospital and she's probably asleep. Is it anything I can help you with, Officer?"

"No, I really need to speak to her, but I can come back."

"No need to do that, I'm Alyx. What's going on?" Alyx had appeared behind Maggie.

"The station received a call shortly after one o'clock this morning about a disturbance at this address. The officer dispatched to the scene found a bedroom window open and no one appeared to be home. Did you notice anything missing?"

"Maggie checked the house a short time ago and I don't think anything is missing."

They both turned to Maggie for confirmation.

"I'm the one who left the window open." Maggie explained what had happened. "We thought that maybe the cats had pushed the screen out and I checked the house. Everything seemed to be in order."

"Two men were found in a van parked down the street, both of them bleeding profusely from scratches and bites—they looked like they had been in a cat fight, but they wouldn't say who did it. We have them in custody on suspicion of wrongdoing. Anything either of you can tell us will help."

"Dogs believe they are human. Cats believe they are God."
—Unknown

CHAPTER THIRTY-ONE: *Unpleasant Memories Revisited*

Alyx stayed in bed the rest of the day and part of the next. Her brother and sister-in-law were there to take care of her needs and ours. Bernice stopped by with food one day, and the next day just to see if she needed anything, giving Maggie a much-needed break.

I stuck as close to Alyx as she allowed. Sunday morning, Alyx's ex, Bob Hille, called to check on her as he promised Ethan he would do.

"I know you hired the lawyer and you don't have to tell me anything, so thank you for authorizing David Hunter to keep me up to date on any new developments and for being there for Ethan. I know it means a lot to him."

There was an awkward silence and Alyx looked uncomfortable.

"I love Ethan and always have, though, I admit, for a while I foolishly lost track of the important things in life. I haven't been much of a father, I know, and I'm sorry for that. I just hope it's not too late to make amends."

"You're right; you have been a jackass, and it has been longer than a while. For his sake, I hope he can forgive you, but only time will tell."

Then Bob told her that the investigation on the theft of her purse had so far led nowhere. I imagined she must have felt helpless. I hoped her outburst hadn't change his mind about keeping her in the loop.

The conversation ended, Alyx tossed off the covers and slid out of bed. "I need to get out of here," she said to no one in particular.

My housemates, anxious to reveal what we knew, started meowing impatiently, swarming around her as she made her way to the bathroom to wash her face and brush her teeth. Clearly distracted by her emotions, she didn't try to figure out what we wanted.

"I need some air. I have to get out of here," she said again.

I realized that it probably wasn't the right time to tell her; there were other things going on that I needed to unravel in order to keep her safe.

"Of all domestic animals, the cat is the most expressive. His face is capable of showing a wide range of expressions. His tail is a mirror of his mind. His gracefulness is surpassed only by his agility. And, along with all these, he has a sense of humor."
—Walter Chandoha

CHAPTER THIRTY-TWO: *The Missing Key*

Alyx went straight to her bedroom when she returned. She showered and washed her hair. Dressed in lounging shorts and a T-shirt, she sat on the couch and promptly fell asleep, waking up when Susan called to see if she needed anything. She mentioned that she hadn't had anything to eat and promised Susan that she would as soon as she got off the phone.

I trotted next to her to the kitchen with the other two following, their tails straight up. Alyx looked around and with a heavy sigh, sat at the kitchen table, across from where she usually sat. It must have been disturbing for her to be sitting there, believing that someone had tried to kill her.

She bent down to pat Misty who was rubbing against her ankles, with Pooky weaving in, out, and around the table legs.

"You all know something is wrong, don't you? I wish you could talk and tell me what happened here Saturday. I bet you know."

I heard a key turn in the lock at the front door. Alyx heard it too. She quickly glanced over to the desk where Maggie had put the house keys and saw there was only one key. I leaped onto the table ready to attack. Alyx took a deep breath and held it until she heard Maggie's voice.

"Alyx, it's me."

"I'm in the kitchen."

"Honey, you're as white as a sheet. Should you be up?"

"I'm fine. You scared me half to death, is all. I saw that one of keys to the new lock was gone and I didn't remember giving you one."

Maggie blushed and stammered an answer. "Well...I just assumed...you wanted me to have a key. I'm sorry for the presumption."

The keys already in her hand, Maggie started to pull off Alyx's house key from her chain, her eyes downcast.

I realized that Alyx knew she had hurt Maggie's feelings. "No, Maggie; I'm the one who's sorry. I shouldn't have said anything."

"I should have called, but I didn't want to wake you in case you were sleeping. I was just going to leave these, if you were. Novie sends her regards and muffins to make you smile."

"How thoughtful of her," she said, taking the bag from Maggie. "You want some?"

"Sure, if you sit and let me make the coffee."

Maggie put two mugs on the table and handed Alyx a plate for the muffins. "Novie has always been nice. She was the first one on our side when we first approached the Downtown Merchants Association about staying open late. Remember?"

"Yes, I do, and she has been on our side on every issue we've discussed since. Do you know what she's decided to do about selling her building?" asked Alyx.

"I think she's getting some pressure from her husband. She says she's still thinking about it."

Maggie poured the coffee and sat down across from Alyx.

"Listen, Maggie, we're partners, but more important, we're friends, and I'm truly sorry I blew up at you and didn't let you explain why you think we should sell and move our business."

"I accept your apology though it's not necessary."

"Thank you for all your help, Maggie. I don't know what would have happened without you here to take care of the cats, the store, and me. And one more thing I want to say is I'm glad you asked Bob to help out; it means a lot to Ethan."

Maggie reached for a muffin and put it on a paper napkin and pushed it over. "Okay, now that's out of the way, how are you feeling? You've lost a some weight; those shorts are a little loose on you."

"I'm okay and so are the shorts as long as they don't fall off."

"How are you emotionally?"

Alyx didn't answer her question directly. She broke a piece off the muffin but didn't put it in her mouth. "Bob called this morning with information on the latest round of non-productive leads. He said the stolen purse lead didn't pan out. The investigator working for the lawyer looked at the store's surveillance video and there was nothing showing the purse being taken, but it did show it being returned by a store employee."

Maggie's eyes opened wide. "Really, that's good isn't it?"

"The employee was questioned and she said she found it on the floor in the produce aisle."

"And they believed her?" Maggie asked, surprised.

"She's a senior citizen who's worked there several years and Bob said there was no reason not to."

"Did Bob say anything else about the case?"

"Just that nothing came out of the other leads either. David told him that in the security video of the parking lot and store entrance, they saw Rupert Moresby enter the coffee shop next to the store right after me. They thought that would lead to something, but it turns out he's just an opportunist and a cheat. He told David he was meeting a woman there."

"The lawyer questioned George Lucas too. Of course, I knew he was wasting his time looking for anything on George. He's as straight as they come," said Maggie.

Alyx hesitated before answering. "I agree, but as far as David was concerned, everyone he talked to could have been a suspect, even you."

Trying for a normalcy I'm sure she didn't feel, Alyx asked, "What's going on with the Swanson account? Were you able to find those circa 1900 pedestal sinks they wanted?"

"I've found two, so far, and I'm waiting to hear from two more dealers."

"Did they agree to use reproductions if we can't find the rest?"

"Yes, but it's really important to them to use original materials as much as possible."

"Did I tell you that I met the former owner, before the house went up for sale?" Alyx asked.

"No, I don't think so."

"She told me that she started the story about the house being haunted. She did it as an advertising gimmick. The story appeared in one of those special sections the paper puts out every so often and the ghost story became part of the history of the house. It never died and she never confessed that she made it up. Just out of curiosity, I asked her if the lie bothered her.

"She said she didn't see why it should since no one could positively say there wasn't a ghost in the house. She said that she did experience some strange things— little things disappearing and then reappearing in strange places and doors opening on their own. She also said that the psychic who came to investigate definitely felt a strange presence in the house. So her point was that maybe there is and maybe there isn't. Who's to say?"

Alyx took a bite of her muffin and smiled. "Have the new owners seen any ghosts, yet?"

Maggie laughed. "Betty told me a funny story the other day. She said she surprised her husband at work one night and practically scared him out of his skin.

He was working in the kitchen and didn't hear her come in. All of a sudden, he saw this huge shadow on the wall. She said he froze to the spot and visibly jumped when she called his name."

The picture of the big tattooed man jumping in fright obviously made the two women laugh.

"Maggie, I'm sorry all this has fallen on your shoulders. Hopefully, I'll be able to come back to work tomorrow or the next day, at least for a few hours anyway."

"You just take your time. I spoke to Charvette and Bernice and they are glad to work the extra hours."

They finished their coffee. Maggie got up to clear the table and continued, "Those two have been so cooperative taking on extra work and more hours, I was thinking about a bonus for them at the end of year. What do you say?"

"I think that's a great idea."

Maggie put the cups in the dishwasher, covered the leftover muffins, and got ready to leave.

Alyx shivered and wrapped her arms around her waist. "It's just starting to sink in that someone tried to hurt me, if not kill me, and I guess I'm feeling a little vulnerable."

"Did something else happen today? Did Bob say something to upset you?"

"It wasn't so much what he said, it was the memories he evoked."

"If you want to talk about it, I have time to listen."

"I've told you most of it already."

"I'm getting older; I may have forgotten some of it, so tell me again so you can expunge it from your mind."

"I don't think I ever told you the details of the night Bob told me he didn't love me anymore and wanted a divorce—the memory, and the aftermath are too painful to recall."

"Time spent with cats is never wasted."—May Sarton

CHAPTER THIRTY-THREE: *Unpleasant Memories*

"Talking with Bob this morning brought back unpleasant memories and coupled with all the bad news, I felt like I was suffocating. The beach always has a calming effect on me, so I dressed and drove to the Inlet Beach. I strolled along the shore and let the painful memories buried a long time ago haunt me for the last time.

"I was so naive back then, I never saw it coming. I truly believed my marriage was solid. We hardly ever argued. Bob was always where he said he would be, and when he wasn't at work, he was with me. I never had a reason to distrust him, yet thinking back, there were a couple of things that happened that should have alerted me, had I not been lulled into a false sense of security. For instance, the strange earring I found on the passenger seat of his car. I could hardly speak when I asked him about it. He was so sure of me, that he didn't even bother to make up a lie. He said he didn't know where it came from, leaving me to draw my own conclusion.

"I rationalized that it could have belonged to a co-worker whom he might have had lunch with. It seemed perfectly innocent—I wasn't worried. Then there was the time he didn't come home from work one night. After he called to say he was going to be late, I didn't hear from him for the rest of the night. Frantic, by the time I finally reached him at work the next morning, he calmly explained that he had spent the night working on a crashed computer program for a client and just wasn't able to call. I let it go for the simple reason I wanted to believe my marriage was solid.

"Then one night, I woke in the early hours of the morning and I was alone in bed. The kitchen light was on, and I went to see if anything was wrong. Bob had been acting restless, and I wondered what was going on. He was sitting on a bar stool at the counter, one hand holding his head, the other holding a lit cigarette. I stood behind him and put my arms around him.

"He loosened my arms and turned to look at me, his soulful eyes begging for pity. 'I don't love you anymore. I want a divorce.' I heard the words but didn't know what they meant.

"'I want a divorce,' he repeated. The words sliced through me to the core. The beautiful, deep blue eyes that warmed my heart had just turned it to ashes. It felt like a nightmare but I knew that it was real.

"'I...don't...understand,' I stammered.

"In an angry tone, he said, 'What's there to understand?' Then, he lowered his voice to almost a whisper, 'I don't love you anymore, I've met someone else—she's my soul mate.'

"I wondered why he was angry since I wasn't the one breaking up the marriage.

"I went back to bed, and curled up on my side of the king-size bed and tried not to think, but the same thoughts kept coming up. What gave him the right to change two people's lives, alter our future—the future I'd depended on for the past eleven years? How did meeting your soul mate negate the promises, the plans, the commitments made to another?

"The next morning, I got up and made breakfast as usual. Everything was the same and nothing was the same. Bob broke Ethan's heart when he told Ethan that he was leaving. He moved out a week later, oblivious to the path of destruction he left behind, leaving me to deal with the damage. But that was a long time ago.

"Anyway, this morning, after a short walk on the beach, I sat on one of the rocks used to form the Inlet jetty—behind me, man's imperfect creation, God's perfect creation in front of me, the blue expanse of the sky meeting the green water of the ocean. The waves lapping at my feet, the rhythm of the pounding surf, the smell of the ocean, the precise formation of the seagulls' flight overhead brought peace to my soul and, after a while, I felt the anxiety begin to melt away until I picked up my towel and headed for the car.

"Then I saw a man I knew when some tourists stopped me to ask directions to the Inlet Lighthouse. I tried my best to avoid him, but he must have picked up his pace and there I was face to face with Dan Ramsey.

'Well, I see you're back among the living,' he said.

I answered, 'Sorry to disappoint you; I was never near death, just sleeping.'

'You'd better be careful, young lady, someone might get serious next time.' He turned his back and headed for the surf.

I didn't want him to know how that had shaken me up and I said, 'You be careful too, Dan. I hear the rip current is pretty strong today.'"

"I think that's exactly what he intended to do, Alyx," replied Maggie, "shake you up. Tell David Hunter about it; see what he thinks, and talk to your brother about it too. I know he wants to help. Of course, if it will make you feel better, I can come and stay with you, or you can stay with me. I know you don't like my sleek modern style—no antiques or shabby furniture in my condo but it does have a view of the ocean just across the street."

"Thank you, Maggie, you've done more than enough already."

Alyx followed her outside and sat in the wicker chair on the porch. "Just last week, my life revolved around the store. This morning when I passed Antiques & Designs on the way to the beach, I didn't stop, didn't even glance in that direction. I've always believed that possessions don't bring lasting happiness, and I'd give it all up in a minute to have my son free."

"Alyx, don't think like that; it's not over for Ethan and if even if it does end badly, the decision can be appealed, new evidence might be found."

"I don't think I can cope with this."

"You'll cope with this the same as you've done before with other things you thought you couldn't handle."

Maggie glanced at her watch, "I hate to leave. Do you want me to stay and keep you company for a while longer?"

"No, I'll be fine. I know we still have a business to run and I want you to keep your appointment with our client."

"Okay. I'll call you later about dinner."

"I'm all set for dinner. Susan called; she's worried I'm not taking care of myself and is dropping something off later."

"I've only spoken to her twice but she seems like a nice person."

"She is. There's only a five-year difference in our ages and we were close friends at one time. Sadly, as time went on, Tom became the focus of her life and her identity. The Susan I knew disappeared; I don't know who she is anymore. At fifty years old, Susan has become the invisible middle-aged woman."

"The reason cats climb is so that they can look down on almost every other animal...it's also the reason they hate birds."
—K. C. Buffington

CHAPTER THIRTY-FOUR: *Loss Of Resolve*

Alyx watched Maggie get in her car, waving as she backed out of the drive. Although the sun was shining and the temperature was in the high seventies, Alyx shivered again. She pulled her cell phone out of her pocket and called her brother who had only recently given her his cell phone number to call in case she needed him.

"Hi, Tom; are you busy?"

She strolled to the end of the driveway, turned around, and looked at the house as if she was seeing it for the first time.

The renovated cottage-style bungalow clad in cedar shingles and clean white trim sat back from the road, the old brick walkway leading to the front porch lined with a variety of annuals and perennials. The blooming azalea bushes across the front of the house reflected the season, and the white wrought-iron settee under the old magnolia tree completed the Southern picture. She waited for Tom on the covered front porch that was just big enough for a white wicker chair and a huge clay pot filled with pink geraniums.

When Tom arrived and asked, "What's wrong? Has something happened?" she burst into tears. He put his arm around her shoulders and helped her inside.

Once in the living room, she wiped her tears with her T-shirt, and, in control again, sat on the couch. Tom sat next to her.

"I used to love this house. Now I'm scared to be in it."

She took a deep breath and told him about the run-in with Ramsey. "Maggie thinks he was just trying to scare me, but it upset me anyway. I'm afraid, Tom. I'm afraid for me because someone tried to kill me, but mostly, I'm afraid for Ethan. Things don't look good for him. What if his lawyer can't convince the jury of his innocence? How can I live my life with my son locked up for something, I know, he didn't do?"

"I've heard really good things about his lawyer. Don't you think he's doing a good job so far?"

"Yes, I do. I trust him, and so does Ethan. I know he'll do the best he can."

"Well, then, give him the chance to do that before you decide it's a lost cause."

"I know you're right, and it does help to hear it from someone else."

"Call the lawyer and tell him about your conversation with Dan Ramsey." He got up to leave and gave her a hug. "I have to keep this appointment. I couldn't postpone it for more than an hour."

He added as an afterthought, "If you're uncomfortable here, why don't you come and stay with us for a while?"

"Thanks for asking, and don't think I don't appreciate it, but I should stay here. I have the cats, and I've imposed on Maggie too much already. Besides, I have to face this too; this is my home and I'm not leaving."

"Okay, take care and call me if you need me. We're family and I love you, even though we don't see much of each other."

She almost started to cry again as she waved good-bye.

"A cat is a lion in a jungle of small bushes."—Indian Proverb

CHAPTER THIRTY-FIVE: *In Their Own Language*

I had convinced the felines—actually, I threatened them with bodily harm—not to do anything foolish when I showed Alyx what happened. Their concern was justified. Alyx would undoubtedly think I was the guilty party but they understood there was no other way. Neither did I have a guarantee that Alyx would understand my message. What I was about to do might just land me in a lot of trouble.

As expected, my loud, guttural yowling propelled Alyx and my housemates to the kitchen to see what was wrong. I gave one big roar, and leaped on the counter, then straight up in the air, just catching the edge of the upper cabinet with my front paws, digging up the side with my back claws. In a perfect replay of what Pooky had said happened, I struggled to hang on and knocked down a basket in the process

Alyx rushed to help, but I pulled myself up, purposefully knocked down another basket, and paused to look at her.

"What's gotten into you, Murfy? Get down from there!" she admonished.

Maggie had told Alyx about my odd behavior with the lawyer and she had probably attributed it to the changes in the household. Now, watching me deliberately knock down another basket, she didn't know what to make of it.

"What is going on here? You get down from there before someone gets hurt."

While she was coaxing me to come down, Misty leaped on the counter on the other side of the sink, onto the refrigerator and lithely up to the top. She gently pushed off a bunch of dried flowers, and before Alyx could do anything, Pooky joined Misty and me. Alyx stepped back, hands on hips, astonished as we continued to push items off, stopping to look at her as the things fell to the counter or to the floor, with a so what are you going to do about it attitude.

She dropped into the nearest chair, flabbergasted at our behavior. The others jumped down—one by one; I defiantly stayed where I was, my eyes boring into hers.

Finally, she got it. She immediately called the number David Hunter had given her, and then sat on the floor.

"This goes way beyond imagination. If I hadn't known better, I would have to say you did that on purpose."

Ethan's lawyer arrived an hour later and Alyx ushered him to the kitchen. If David Hunter thought it strange when he saw all the items on the floor, he didn't say so.

"You sounded sure when you said you knew what happened. What did you remember?"

"Actually, my cats told me what happened."

He looked at her askew. "Your cats talk to you?"

"Yes, cats do talk when humans are willing to listen. True, their native tongue is body language, but house cats have developed a wide variety of meows intended to alert humans to their needs and intentions. Sometimes I get the feeling that Murfy can read my mind, and lets me know what he wants me to know is going on in his. I think it's just a lucky guess when I get it right, but who knows?"

"So what did they tell you?"

"They didn't tell me anything. They helped me figure out that what happened was an accident.

"The first time you asked me to tell you what happened, I said I was sitting at the kitchen table and the cats were being cats. What I meant by that was that they were eating, sleeping or chasing something around.

"When I came back to the kitchen from checking out the noise in the guestroom, I saw one of those green lizards you see everywhere frantically climbing the wall and, because of the sounds I heard in the living room earlier, I thought one of the cats must have been after it. Usually, I rescue them from the cats, but this one seemed safe, so I paid no more attention."

The quizzical look on Hunter's face must have irritated her as much as it did me.

"Don't you see? One of the cats must have been stalking it, jumped up there and accidentally knocked down the pot that hit me."

"Those lizards are called Green Anole and that's pretty high for a cat to jump. Did they ever do that before?"

"I've never seen them do it, but that doesn't mean they haven't done it in the past."

His skepticism was annoying, and what did Alyx care about the proper name of the lizard?

"Do you have any cats?" she asked.

"No."

"Have you ever spent any time with cats?"

Again, he responded with a negative and at the same time backed into the closest chair.

"So you don't know anything about them. Well, I have three. They do things that can make you crazy if you try to figure it out. Cats aren't show-offs, and you have no idea what they can do until they do it."

Her cheeks turned red when his mouth twitched, holding back a smile or maybe laughter, infuriating her even more.

She sat across from him and he turned to face her.

"Okay, how did they do it? How did they get to the top of the cabinets?"

"Misty went by way of the refrigerator. The other two went floor to counter and straight up. Murfy almost didn't make it and knocked down a basket in the process.

"Don't you see—it could have happened just like that. It's bizarre, I know, but I read an article in the newspaper some time back, about a man shot in the rear by his cat while he was standing at the stove cooking his breakfast. The article said that he had placed his loaded handgun on the counter and his cat had accidentally knocked it off, causing it to fire. And that, you can find in the paper's archives, I'm sure."

"I agree it's a paw-sible theory but..."

She looked away hiding a smile. "You called it a *paw-sible* theory."

"I know you want to help your son and believe me, so do I. As I said, it's a plausible theory, but it isn't enough to convince anyone. The prosecutor will focus on the witness account of Ethan arriving here ten minutes before Maggie saw him. We need proof that Ethan was at the convenience store buying cat treats. What we need is that receipt with the date and time on it. Ethan doesn't know if the receipt was in the bag and he doesn't remember seeing it fall out of the bag, and Maggie didn't see it either."

That was my cue and I had it covered. I snaked my paw under the stove, meowing desperately. Alyx shot out of her seat and dropped to her knees, stretching her hand under the stove, and didn't feel anything. Hunter suggested removing the bottom drawer of the stove, an easy task made more difficult by all of us crowding around.

The drawer came out and there it was. Alyx grabbed Hunter's arm and squeezed as he scrutinized the receipt. A broad grin spread across his face. The time printed on the receipt proved Ethan innocent without a doubt. Alyx laughed and cried all at the same time.

Hunter cleared his throat, "Next time I have a tough case, I'll hire you and your team to investigate."

"You mean Murfy and his team; I was just the interpreter in this case."

"Murfy is a very clever cat; where did you get him?"

Alyx told him the story as she walked him through the living room on his way out. Hunter sat his briefcase down and leaned against the back of my favorite chair.

"My next-door neighbor, Joann, told me about the kittens. The owner hadn't advertised the free kittens for fear they might be abused or used for experiments, so she was trying to place them through word of mouth.

"I remember the day I rang the doorbell with a little excitement and a lot of trepidation. I promised Ethan he could have a pet and decided that a cat would be a better fit for our lifestyle, but wasn't sure, if I truly wanted the added responsibility or the extra expense involved in keeping a pet.

"A pleasant, attractive woman wearing a sari, and cradling a white Persian cat in her arms, answered the door.

"I introduced myself and she said she was expecting me.

"'I'm Brenda, by the way, and this is Duchess, the kitten's mother. I don't know who the father is, but he must have been a good-looking tomcat. Wait until you see the kittens.'

"When she said that, Duchess catapulted out of her arms and ran ahead. 'She's a calm, affectionate cat, but very protective of her babies.'

"Brenda didn't exaggerate about the kittens; they looked like the most adorable stuffed animals—soft and furry. They all stopped playing and looked up when I walked in, but only one of them—a longhaired, cream tabby ran to me without hesitation when I went down on my knees.

"Under his mother's watchful eyes, I gently lifted the kit, and he nestled under my chin, stealing my heart.

"I wondered which one Joan had picked and Brenda said she was still working on convincing her husband that they needed a cat.

"I asked if that meant I could choose any one of them. She said it was clear that the kitten had already made his choice. And so he had. He was the biggest and the spunkiest of the litter, and Brenda said that he seemed to be a natural born leader judging from the way the others followed his lead.

"I was sure Ethan was going to love the tough little guy. I put him down and watched him practice his hide-wait and pounce technique on one of the other kittens, before he started gnawing on a plastic straw. When I said, "I'll see you soon, kitty, he sealed the deal with a tiny "mew." At the time, I foolishly thought I was the one who did the choosing—little did I know."

"I promised Brenda I'd mention the kittens to everyone I knew and I did."

"Did she find a home for all of them?" asked Hunter.

"I was happy to hear that she did eventually."

"Well, I'd better go and start working on bringing Ethan home."

Hunter reached for his briefcase, glancing at the patio door as he straightened up. He commented on the pet door, drawing Alyx's attention to the propped open screen door. Alyx explained that Pooky got out during all the commotion with the ambulance and the police and Maggie left the door propped open for her to come in when she got hungry.

"Has Murfy figured out how to open the cat door yet?"

She looked at him funny. "No, but I did see him fooling around with it soon after it was installed."

"I suggest you keep an eye on it."

He said it in jest, and they both laughed. I didn't see any humor in it. I lost some of my freedom when Alyx closed and locked the screen door.

"Of all God's creatures, there is only one that cannot be made slave of the leash. That one is the cat."—Mark Twain

CHAPTER THIRTY-SIX: *One of a Kind*

She had nothing to do but wait. The hands on the antique mantle clock didn't seem to be moving fast enough. Hunter had called early that morning and told her that the judge had signed the release papers.

"It looks like I'll have to bring that clock to the repair shop," she said with a heavy sigh.

Sitting innocently at her feet, I looked up and gave her a short meow.

"You're right, Murfy; there's nothing wrong with the clock. I'm anxious, is all," she admitted, "I can't wait for Ethan to get home. Thanks to you, David is on his way to the County Branch jail right now to pick him up."

She smiled, probably thinking that anyone hearing her talking to her pet would think she'd lost her mind, but if that's the case, there's lots of crazy folks out there.

When finally, Ethan walked in, we were all so happy to see the radiant smile on Alyx's face that Misty didn't even pester Ethan for cat treats. We were totally surprised when he pulled out our favorite from his pocket.

The following day was Alyx's first official day back to work; I followed her to the two-year old truck, jumped in when she opened the door and wedged myself under the passenger seat.

"Come on, Murfy; I have to get to work. Maggie needs me," she said, grabbing my back foot and gently tugging. I'd wrapped my paws around something solid under there and I held on tight. She pulled and I protested loudly.

"Okay, cat, you win, but you won't have the run of the place like you think you will. I don't want to worry about you running out every time someone comes in or goes out."

I knew what that meant. A few minutes later, she came back out from the house, loaded with necessities, including the much-hated harness and leash. I hissed, she laughed, my roommates watched from the house, horrified.

"Hey, don't hiss at me—it was your idea to come, remember?"

It was a short ride to Antiques & Designs, and I was only slightly hyperventilating. Alyx had called on the way, and Maggie was waiting for us at the back door.

"Since we have another half-hour before we open, let's leave Murfy free to explore the store. It's been a long time since he was here last. It will give him a chance to get reacquainted with the surroundings, and then I'll put the harness and leash on him."

"That should be fun," Maggie said, laughing "If I remember right, you didn't have him on a leash the last time he was here."

"That was because the store was closed—as it is now. I'll take it off when I'm sure he'll stay put without it."

"Did he ever let you put him on a leash before?"

"When we first moved in and before I had the back porch screened. He gave me a hard time at first, but as smart as he is, he quickly figured out that if he wanted to be outside, he would have to be on a lead. I only had to do that a couple of times, and then he just started to stay close and I let him free.

"I remembered that was also the first time he met Smooch, the Pomeranian next door—his first encounter with a dog. Murfy was exploring the bushes a few feet away from me, and without any warning, Smooch came charging across the lawn barking raucously, as small dogs often do. The dog meant business, and I feared for Murfy's safety and mine.

"Murfy is roughly the same size as the dog, but when he puffed out his fur, he look twice as big. He strutted towards the dog, ready to rumble. Smooch stopped in his tracks, turned and went running back to his home, his tail tucked between his legs. He had obviously had other encounters with cats and had learned his lesson. Murfy held his position until the dog left his territory, then swaggered back, and nonchalantly draped himself across my feet."

I remembered that day as well. My mother didn't have time to teach me much, but the first thing she taught me was that although it's not true that dogs and cats are natural enemies, some dogs do hate us just because we're cats and will attack on sight. She said our claws gave us the advantage, and I needed to be judicious about using them. Well, I didn't have claws, so I bluffed. Smooch is a simple dog and was just as scared to get into a fight as I was and it had worked.

Closely observed by Maggie, I cautiously set off to investigate the store with a sniff here, a taste there—rubbing against some pieces of furniture to mark them mine, while gingerly touching other things with my paws in order to determine if they were friend or foe.

"You know, Alyx," said Maggie, "it might be fun to have him around. He lends an air of hominess to the place, don't you agree?"

"I do. It will be interesting to see how our customers react," she answered as they both went about the business of getting ready for the day.

"Don't buy a cat in a bag."—Unknown

CHAPTER THIRTY-SEVEN: *Back To Work*

The first item on Alyx's list of things to do that morning was to thank Novie Moresby for her willingness to testify for Ethan. The short article in the newspaper about Ethan's release, and his statement about the part that the female cats and I had played in solving the case and preventing a murder made me an instant celebrity. For the most part, the customers loved having me around, and I sort of liked being there. I was still worried about Alyx though, so when she was ready to leave to go see Novie, I put up such a fuss that she thought it best to bring me with her.

Novie greeted Alyx with a smile and a hug.

"I hope you're okay with the cat," said Alyx to her next door neighbor. "He's on a leash and I know he won't be a problem." The last part was said directly to me just in case I had other ideas.

"It's fine," Novie smiled, "I'm so glad to see you back to work. You look great."

She directed Alyx to an empty table in the rear of the café and asked the server to bring two coffees and muffins.

"Novie, I just want you to know how much I appreciate your willingness to testify for Ethan."

"I'm glad everything worked out," Novie replied. "I can only imagine how awful this whole experience has been for both of you."

"Honestly, no parent should have to experience what I just went through. I felt so helpless, you know, everything was against him. Ethan's life was in the hands of strangers who didn't know him. True, they had some factual information about him, but they didn't know him like I do."

All of Alyx's emotions were now out in the open as she continued, "They knew about his financial problems and they believed that was his motive for wanting to kill me. I won't make excuses for his fiscal irresponsibility, but I understand.

No one really knows how rough it was for Ethan when he was young. I was working for minimum wage. What I made, plus the small child support payment from his father, allowed me to meet our needs, but not our wants. Although, like every parent, I wanted to give Ethan the world, I refused to go into debt for our wants. Ethan had to settle for whatever was on sale. Toys, and, later, the more expensive things like skateboards and surfboards came from garage sales. In this commercial driven world, it's hard for a child to understand why they can't have the latest toys, or the hot new bike like their friends have. A teenager may understand why they can't buy the designer clothes at the mall, or the two hundred dollar pair of athletic shoes and why they have to settle for whatever is on sale, but it doesn't make it any easier for them."

She paused and took a sip of coffee. "I'm sorry, Novie, you probably don't want to hear any of this. I didn't mean to get into it," and, steering the conversation in another direction, she asked Novie if she had given any more thought to selling her building.

"I really haven't decided yet. Rupert is pressuring me to sell, but owning this café is something I've wanted for a long time and I'm just not sure I want to sell." She looked around the room, her face reflecting the pride she felt.

"My parents struggled to make a living, starting with a small grocery store and eventually buying this building twenty-years ago," said Novie. "My father was the first African-American to buy commercial property outside of the black community they lived in."

"I understand completely," replied Alyx. "It took a lot of hard work and sacrifice for Maggie and me to buy our building and make our business a success. Maggie doesn't really want to sell either, but she thought we should talk about it. Poor Maggie; I feel so strongly about what we've accomplished that I'm afraid I got mad at her for even thinking about selling."

Then Alyx brought up the Merchant's Association meeting and asked Novie what she thought of the idea of hosting the Annual Arts Festival. Novie thought it was a great idea and, as usual, promised to support Alyx and Maggie when the issue came up at the next meeting. Alyx saw that the restaurant was starting to get busy, so she finished her coffee and they said their good-byes. I got a pat on the head from Novie and some quizzical looks from customers as we left the restaurant.

We returned to the store. The second item on Alyx's list of things to do was talk to Maggie about having a celebration dinner. Maggie thought it was a great idea, and suggested that they invite David Hunter, as well, and so Alyx did just that.

She phoned Hunter at his office and invited him to dinner the following Friday at the best French restaurant in the area. He said he lived near there and would be happy to meet the group at the restaurant at seven.

Maggie walked in the office just as Alyx was returning the phone to its cradle.

"You're all flushed. What's the matter, did someone give you a hard time?"

"Well, no, not exactly. I was just talking to David Hunter, inviting him to dinner Friday, and well, I just got a little flustered, that's all."

"Oh, you just got a little flustered, did you now?" teased Maggie.

"I was doing just fine until he said he didn't have a wife, or a girlfriend," she laughed. I don't know if he's married. I don't believe he is. At any rate, I don't remember seeing a wedding band, but I thought I should invite his wife in case he was, and he gave me an ambiguous answer. He said he wasn't currently living with one. Now, what does that mean?"

"I suppose," said Maggie with a sly smile, "that it could mean he's either separated or in the process of getting a divorce, but it could also mean he's not married."

Maggie poured a cup of coffee and sat across from Alyx. "That's a typical lawyer answer, isn't it? Speaking of married men, has Charvette ever talked to you about a boyfriend?"

"Not in so many words, but judging from some of the things she says, I assume she has been seeing someone."

"Don't you find it strange," posed Maggie, "that he's never picked her up for lunch, though we know from her actions and what she says, she's had lunch with him before? And how about those afternoons when she takes off for a couple of hours and comes back positively glowing?"

"I know what you mean," responded Alyx, scowling. "You don't suppose she's seeing a married man, do you?"

"Of course, it's none of our business as her employers but yes, I think it's possible, and she doesn't want us to know who it is."

"Then it's probably someone we know. Don't you think?"

"It could be but it would surprise me; she's too smart to get involved with a married man," noted Alyx, then she added, "Anyway, at Charvette's age, she should know better."

"You're right," agreed Maggie, "but some women never learn, believing the situation is different for them—and sometimes it is." She said this last with a slight sigh.

Maggie then said she had an appointment, but before she left, she asked Alyx if she had dinner plans.

"No, why?"

"Let's try that new place down the street. I hear the owner is really good-looking!"

Alyx couldn't help but smile, "How about the food?"

"Oh, I hear that's real good too," she answered, not missing the good-natured dig.

"No, heaven will not ever heaven be; unless my cats are there to welcome me."—Unknown

CHAPTER THIRTY-EIGHT: *A Blooming Romance*

Alyx was sitting in a wing chair by the store's front door, taking a break while contemplating something. She looked up when a customer walked in, smiled and said, "Take your time looking around, I'll be right here if you need anything," and made no move to get up, allowing the customer the freedom to look around at her leisure.

The older woman hesitantly smiled back and moved away, heading directly towards Alyx's favorite English antique—a late eighteenth century George III, slant-front desk on display in the front window. The inlaid oak desk had a narrow rectangular top above a hinged slant top, opening to a gilt-tooled leather writing surface. A variety of small drawers and pigeonholes flanked a central banded door. It had four long, graduated, and inlay-banded drawers with pierced batwing brasses.

About five minutes later, the woman was still admiring the desk, lovingly running her hands over the surface. Holding on to me, Alyx approached the customer.

"This is my favorite piece, too," Alyx said, looking at the woman who appeared to be in her early seventies with short, silvery hair and a pink complexion. She spoke in an odd way, somewhat hesitantly. "I used to have a desk like this one in my home. I had to leave it behind when we moved back to America. How did you acquire the desk?"

"I found it at an estate sale," replied Alyx. "It was my understanding that the woman who owned it had brought it back from Africa."

For just a moment, the woman's eyes seemed to glaze over, and then she looked at me.

"He's a handsome cat, isn't he? I have a lovely cat at home," she said, reaching out to scratch my ear.

"What kind is it and what's his name?" Alyx asked.

"He's a Siamese and his name is Simon," she said affectionately. Her gaze went back to the desk. "I probably can't afford it, but how much is it?"

"We're asking two thousand five hundred," answered Alyx, almost apologetically.

"That's more than I can spend right now. Maybe someday…"

"Is there anything else I can show you?"

"No. I saw that piece in the window and I just wanted to take a closer look. I would like to wander about, if you don't mind."

"Sure. As you can see, we have many nice things to look at. By the way, my name is Alyx Hille; I'm part owner of the store. Please feel free to come back and visit anytime."

"Thank you, Alyx, and my name is Althea Burns."

Other customers had entered the store, and Alyx saw one of them looking around for assistance, so she headed in that direction. When she had an opportunity, she looked around again for Althea and saw that she was gone. Alyx walked over to the desk the woman had been admiring, scratched out the price and wrote "Sold" on the tag. Maggie would understand.

The rest of the day was a busy one. The variety of people I encountered fascinated me. Some ignored me and others put up too much of a fuss, wanting to pet me or hold me. When I couldn't take it anymore, I hid under the counter. At one point, I came out from behind the counter just in time to see a heavyset man about sixty with dark button eyes peering in the window—it was Dan Ramsey.

Alyx and Maggie didn't get a chance to speak again until Maggie came back to the store around dinnertime.

"I stopped in at Angelo's on the River to make reservations for later today but they close at five today," said Maggie. "The restaurant is fancier than other restaurants on Ocean Street; it actually has starched, white linen tablecloths and real flowers on the tables. Charlie, the owner, looks like the hero on the cover of a lusty romance novel. His voice is as gentle as a breeze. 'Are you ready to be seated or are you waiting for someone?' Yikes, Alyx! He's gorgeous. And when he smiled—he has these perfect white teeth in a perfectly tanned face. I was totally tongue-tied and could barely answer his easy question. He said to be sure and come back another time."

"Why does he call the restaurant Angelo's if his name is Charlie?" Alyx asked.

"I asked him that too—between drools. The short answer is that his father's name is Angelo and evidently a much more descriptive name for an Italian restaurant. He seemed nice," Maggie said with a wink.

"And very savvy about marketing," noted Alyx. "He's just what we need on our side."

"I mentioned to him that we're the owners of Antiques & Designs down the street and we hoped to see him at the Downtown Merchants Association meeting next month. I said that you and I are going to propose that we get involved in sponsoring community events such as the Annual Arts Festival usually held at Beachside Community College, and that we've already spoken with the key organizers, and they're very enthusiastic about moving it downtown."

"Did he have any thoughts on it?"

"He said it sounded like a good idea and looked forward to hearing more about it at the meeting."

Alyx smiled broadly. "Well, it should be an interesting one," she said.

"He asked if we expected some resistance. I said, 'let's just say not all merchants on Ocean Street share our same vision, and leave it at that."

"That's good," added Alyx, "we can use another business on our side."

"So...it was too late for dinner," said Maggie, "but he said there was time for a take-out order just because we're neighbors and also so we'll recommend the restaurant to our customers."

"Did they have eggplant cannelloni on the menu?"

"Yes, they did," replied Maggie. "I ordered that for you and chicken Alfredo for me. I said I'd pick-up the order at closing."

"You're coming to my house. Right?"

"Yes, if you don't mind, that way the food will still be hot when we sit down to eat."

After dinner that evening, the two women moved to the living room, and the girls and I finished the leftovers in the kitchen. Yum! I meandered out to listen to their conversation, my tummy delightfully full.

"Maggie, that was the best Italian food I've had in a long time."

"I'm glad this worked out, and I'm glad you're back home," said Maggie. "I've wanted to talk to you about something."

Alyx was puzzled. "What is it, Maggie?"

"Well," she began, lowering her head and looking up shyly, "How do you feel about George?"

"George who?"

"What do you mean George who? Our George. George Lucas—the man who creates those wonderful things for us," Maggie answered, somewhat exasperated.

"Oh, yes. Well, you know George is a friend. I've known him for years, and I think he's a very nice man. Why? What's going on?"

"Nice. That's all you have to say about him?"

Alyx was puzzled. "Well, he's no Charlie," she whispered as she leaned forward. "At least, not from your description." She giggled.

I saw something flicker on Maggie's face, maybe hurt feelings, but I wasn't sure.

"So…what about George?" Alyx asked.

Maggie bit her lower lip. "He asked me out to dinner. I accepted, but I'm not sure I should have."

"George is a good man," said Alyx, "solid as a rock but very shy. He's the kind of man easily forgotten, until you get to know him better. According to what I know about you, Maggie, George isn't your type at all and I'm surprised you even considered dating him."

"Alyx, I haven't told you all there is to tell about my failed marriages. I'm not good at analyzing my actions, but I think it was because I was embarrassed; you've always had such a high opinion of me that I didn't want you to know what a fool I really was."

"We've all done foolish things, and not necessarily all of them in our youth. Believe me, Maggie, I'm the last one to throw stones."

"I met my first husband the summer I graduated high school," said Maggie. "Swept off my feet by his charm and good looks. I married him against my parent's wishes. It didn't matter to me that he didn't have a job, I did, and I thought he could get one later. In fact, he did get several jobs, none of them good enough for him.

I didn't mind putting my college plans on hold while he *explored* the possibilities. My parents were modestly well off but refused to help during the hard times, disliking their son-in-law and not having forgiven me for going against their wishes. Two years later, he was still *exploring* and I was still supporting him.

"One evening, more charming and better looking than ever, he took me out to dinner to celebrate the new job he had landed and announced he had met someone else—his soul mate.

"I wasn't quite over him when I met another charming, handsome man, looking for a generous, good-hearted woman just like me. I told myself this one was different—he had a steady job and ambition.

"A few months after we were married, he quit his job and started school full time. I had nothing to complain about—he made me happy. The following year, my parents died in a car accident. What they left me helped provide a comfortable lifestyle while he finished school, and to establish his law practice when he graduated. Ten years later, he told me he had outgrown me—he had found his soul mate.

"So you see, George may not be handsome or charming, but he has substance and integrity and I value those qualities above all else."

"George is one of the kindest men I've ever met," agreed Alyx. "I think you should keep seeing him and see where it goes."

After dinner, Alyx and Maggie stayed in the kitchen talking and the females and I went out on the lanai. The girls wanted to hear about my experience that day at the store, and Misty wanted to know why I went in the first place. She said they had speculated about it all day and hadn't agreed on anything.

I hesitated, not sure if I should, and then went ahead and told them the truth. I had this nagging suspicion that not everything had been resolved. I didn't know exactly what was wrong—nothing specific, anyway.

I reminded them that prior to Ethan's release, I had heard talk about condominiums and selling Antiques & Designs and the café next-door. The conversation between Alyx and Novie, the owner of the café, had convinced me that matters were still undecided. I said to the females that we needed to look after Alyx for a while longer and asked for their help in keeping her safe—and that meant going to the store. Misty enthusiastically agreed. Pooky reluctantly agreed but only when and if necessary.

That settled, I told them the day had gone better than I had expected. The short article in the newspaper about Ethan's release, and his statement about the part we played in solving the case had made me an immediate celebrity. Everybody knew I was the same Murfy that was mentioned in the article. As far as I could tell, most of the customers liked having me around.

I told them about all the things to climb on, places to hide and perfect places for catnaps. I also told them the best part of the day was when customers dropped treats and toys in the big basket on the counter.

I didn't tell them that the first customer to spot me was not an animal lover. When she saw me curled up in a rocking chair near the checkout counter, she had snorted indignantly at the idea of an animal in the store, let alone one sitting on a piece of furniture she might want to buy. I heard her comments and didn't consider her worthy of my attention, not even when she made a remark about animals keeping to their place. The little girl with her had similar sentiments. She sneaked up behind the rocker and pulled my tail. Infuriated by her action, my tail flicked wildly, my slanted eyes and flattened ears delivering a powerful message. The little girl instinctively ran off and joined her mother who had moved away. When that had happened, I wondered if I'd made a mistake forcing Alyx to bring me to the store, but I decided I just needed to choose my napping places a little more carefully in the future.

"I like pigs. Pigs look up to us. Cats look down on us. Pigs treat us as equals."— Winston Churchill

CHAPTER THIRTY-NINE: *The Bodyguards*

The next day, Misty, Pooky, and I pushed our way out the door as Alyx was leaving and gave her a hard time herding us back into the house. After picking up a few more harnesses and leashes, she piled us in two carriers and we left, Pooky complaining all the way because she had to share her carrier with Misty.

Maggie was right about having resident cats. Most of the customers loved the idea and started bringing enough treats to warrant a basket on the counter to hold all the goodies.

For the most part, the other two stayed away from the customers. I preferred to stay close to the entrance and scrutinize the customers as they walked in. Every so often, someone came in who didn't smell right and I followed that one around the store unseen. Bernice said that she thought cats had a sense of right and wrong, and knew when someone was not to be trusted and she was right. Unfortunately, that was really all I had.

I found out from Pooky's snitches, that the condominium deal between Dunne and Moresby was a legitimate business deal. Hunter vouched for Dunne's honesty. I still didn't trust Moresby. He wouldn't give the woman's name who he was meeting at the coffee shop when Alyx's purse was stolen, so his story couldn't be confirmed.

Mid-morning, Alyx's customer, Althea Burns stepped through the door and went straight to the slant-front desk she had admired earlier that week. The elderly woman expressed her disappointment at the "Sold" sign when Alyx greeted her.

"I see you sold the desk already. I'm not surprised; it's such a beautiful piece," she said, lovingly running her hands over the top.

"Actually, it's not sold. I just decided to hold on to it for a while," Alyx said, watching Althea's peaches and cream complexion brighten at the news.

"Since there isn't much activity going on this morning, would you like to join me for coffee at the café next door? Do you have time? They have wonderful homemade muffins and all kinds of coffees and teas."

"Well, yes, that would be nice. I don't drink coffee, but I would like to have a cup of tea."

"Great. Let me tell Charvette where I'm going and that I'll be right back."

I followed discreetly behind the two women, slipping into the café alongside them. Novie greeted us warmly and led us to a booth overlooking the marina.

"I see you have your bodyguard with you again," said Novie.

"Oh, yes; he's put it in his head that he has to be with me every minute of the day," said Alyx.

Alyx then introduced Althea, and Novie said she'd send someone right over. After the women were served, Alyx got down to questioning.

"Tell me about your desk, Althea. Where and when did you buy it?" asked Alyx, cutting her apple muffin in half.

"My husband bought the desk for me on our honeymoon. We were married in London and honeymooned in Sierra Leone, Africa, where he had a job as overseer in a diamond counting house."

"What do they do in a counting house, count diamonds?"

"In a fashion. A counting house is where they sort rough diamonds according to their size. My husband, Paul, was a collector of sorts and enjoyed going to auctions, which is where we found a desk just like the one in your shop."

"I understand your attraction. I feel the same way about that piece and some others I have in my home—pieces I don't think I could part with."

"In my case, it wasn't just the desk. It was the romantic story associated with it that touched a young bride's heart. The story was that a poor young man had fallen in love with the daughter of a rich diamond mine executive, who forbade the relationship. They say the young man stole a diamond and brought it to her to let her know that now they had enough money to run away and get married. She held the diamond in her hand when the company guards burst in and killed him. They said she hid the diamond in a secret compartment built into the desk. She never married and kept the desk in her room till she died. My husband and I attended the auction where I saw the desk, and when I saw the same one in your shop, a flood of memories from that time came back to me. You see my husband just passed away four months ago."

"I'm sorry about your husband."

"Don't be. He was very ill and it was for the best."

"Althea, if you want the desk, we can make arrangements for the payment."

"No, dear; I don't buy things on credit, especially sentimental things. I'll have the money soon enough. It won't be long before everything is settled."

Alyx was fascinated by the stories about Althea's life in Africa and told her she would invite her business partner Maggie to join them the next time she stopped in.

"Thank you so much for this unexpected treat. Novie is a lovely woman, and her muffins are everything you said they were. Mostly, thank you for spending a little time with an old lady. I truly enjoyed myself."

"You're an interesting woman, and I enjoyed talking to you."

When we returned to the store, David Hunter was standing at the checkout counter. He looked a little nervous and I wondered what was going on. I hoped he hadn't come to tell Alyx he couldn't make it to dinner. That would disappoint Alex.

Alyx was wearing jeans and a simple, unadorned T-shirt. She smiled when she saw Hunter and his face lit up as if he'd received the best gift ever.

"Hello, David. It's good to see you. Are you still coming to my dinner party?"

"Yes, definitely. I'm looking forward to it. It will be good to see Ethan again with a smile on his face, I'm sure."

"I was really worried about him, David. I was happy that you were able to get his case dismissed so quickly."

"I'm glad it all worked out."

"What brings you here today, work, or pleasure?"

"Definitely pleasure," he answered, maybe a little quickly. "The last time I was here, I saw a bronze statue I thought would look good in my office, if you still have it."

"The scales-of-justice?"

"Yes, you still have it?"

"I think so," she said, looking around.

He followed her to the other side of the store and carried the bronze back to the checkout counter. Alyx wrote out the sales slip and David took out his credit card.

"Is that it for today?"

"There's just one more thing. I have a small collection of law books, and I was wondering if you could help me locate a rare first edition book I've had trouble finding."

"Books are not my area of expertise, but I know a book dealer, Joe Borando, owner of The Book Room, a large store that deals in antiquarian, rare, and collectible books.

She grabbed a small pad of paper from the end of the counter and reached for a pen, poised to write down the information.

"Here, let me write it down for you," he said taking the pen from her.

"It sounds fascinating," she said tongue-in-cheek when she read what he'd written.

"What makes it even more scintillating, it's a landmark of jurisprudence," he answered in kind.

The transaction completed, she handed him the wrapped package. "I'll let you know if I find that book you want."

"I know this is short notice, but are you free for lunch as an advanced thank you for helping me find the book? If you're busy, we can do it another time."

"Lunch sounds great," Alyx said. "You want me to meet you somewhere?"

"How about that new place, Angelo's? I hear the food is excellent."

"I haven't been there, but they have take-out, and I agree the food is excellent. The restaurant is actually owned and operated by a real Italian, unlike most of the other Italian restaurants in the area."

"Alright then. Is one o'clock a good time?"

"One thirty would be better."

"Great. I'll see you then, Alyx."

"Yes, you will," she said.

Hunter left without further ceremony. I happened to catch Charvette looking at her, and what I saw in her eyes made my fur stand up. Alyx must have seen it too. She told Charvette she'd be in her office doing some catchup chores and to come get her if it got busy.

"If animals could speak, the dog would be a blundering outspoken fellow, but the cat would have the rare grace of never saying a word much."—Mark Twain

CHAPTER FORTY: *Search for First Edition Law Book*

The next day, Maggie stopped in to pick-up something she had forgotten and needed for a client.

"How did lunch with David go yesterday?" she asked. "Did he clarify what he meant about a wife or a girlfriend?"

"How do you know I had lunch with David?"

"I called while you were out and Charvette told me."

"Our impromptu lunch turned out to be a very pleasant affair for the most part. The conversation flowed easily, with neither of us running out of things to say. We kept the conversation on a general level, deliberately staying away from discussing anything personal, but by the end of the meal, I felt the tension that had built up in just sticking to general conversation. Then he said something I don't know how to take. He apologized for offending me for what he called an unprofessional lapse—referring to our first meeting when he had put his hand over mine, barely making contact, and then removing it as if burned. He said he did it because I looked so sad he just wanted to bring me comfort."

"Were you offended?"

"No, I took it as he meant it—a kind gesture. So what's the big deal, do you suppose?"

"Maybe it meant something else to him—maybe he never does that no matter how sad and vulnerable his clients may look."

"Anyway, we shook hands at the store's door. He said he enjoyed lunch, and looked forward to seeing Ethan at my dinner party, and that was it."

"You didn't ask if he's married?"

"Like I said, we didn't talk about anything personal. He said lunch was an advance thank you for helping him find a first edition book he wants for his collection; it didn't seem appropriate to ask."

The rest of the day was uneventful. Customers were few and Alyx spent most of her time in the office. She called someone using her laptop and I could see him on her screen. After chatting for a few minutes, she asked the man to locate the book David had wanted.

"You don't happen to have it on your shelves, do you?"

"No, not that one. I do have a couple of other law books, though. It would make me very happy if I could interest him in one of them."

"Just out of curiosity, how much?"

"They're both first editions, one is five hundred dollars and the other is one thousand dollars."

"Wow, I had no idea."

"You think that's a lot of money, there's an Internet site that lists law books with prices ranging from one dollar to ten million."

"What is a first edition, anyway?"

"A first edition is a copy of a book printed from the first setting of type. It's the first time the text appears in public in that form."

"And how do you know it's a first edition?"

"Well, that can be one of the most difficult aspects of collecting. One of the keys is to verify that the book is at least a first printing. A number line on the copyright page often indicates this, with the lowest number being the printing."

"I know you deal in both antiquarian and rare books. What's the difference?"

"Antiquarian refers to collecting older/antique books. The age of a book has very little to do with its value, by the way. Dealers and collectors consider factors like intrinsic importance, condition, and demand."

"Do you think it will take you long to find this particular book for my friend?"

"It depends, if my usual sources don't have it, I'll try the Internet. Sometimes I can have it in a week and sometimes it takes months for a book to turn up."

"Well, he's been looking a long time for it, and I'm sure he won't mind waiting a little longer."

"Hey, not to change the subject," said the man on the screen with a saucy tip of his head, "but changing the subject, I'm going to be out your way on business in a couple of weeks, how about getting together for dinner?"

"You ask me that every time I talk to you. I'm truly flattered but I don't think I can," said Alyx.

"And that's what you say every time I ask."

"So why do you keep asking?"

"I keep hoping you'll change your mind."

"Call me when you find the book, and I'll let you know about dinner."

I already knew what her answer was going to be. She had asked Ethan once what he thought about her dating a younger man. He said it would only bother him if the guy were close to his own age. Although it's difficult to tell someone's age these days, this guy didn't look a lot older than Ethan did, maybe ten to fifteen years older.

After this Internet chat, I figured Alyx was safe in the office for a while, so I went back out on the floor to

188 *A Paw-sible Theory*

make my rounds and check on my housemates who were also on the lookout for anything unusual. I expected foul play from one of three suspects: Rupert Moresby, Dan Ramsey, or Charvette.

After Pooky's friend Jemma had reported that according to James Dunne, Novie had decided not to sell, I figured one of them was going to make a move soon.

"It always gives me a shiver when I see a cat seeing what I can't see."—Eleanor Farjeon

CHAPTER FORTY-ONE: *The Cats Help Prevent a Murder*

The next day, Alyx moved a couple of pieces of light furniture away from the entrance and unlocked the door before Charvette arrived. Maggie had taken a couple of well-deserved days off to spend with George and Bernice had called in sick, so it was just the two of them and the three of us in the store. I instructed the girls to be on the lookout for a walrus mustache, and black button eyes, although I wasn't sure of what or even if anything was going to happen. That meant no napping. They didn't like that and I had to remind them that our job was to help our humans.

"The weather report I heard before I left the house said nothing about rain today…it sure looks like rain to me," said Charvette, sounding a little angry about it.

"Personally," said Alyx, "I think the weather people try to put a positive spin on the weather so as not to scare the tourists from going out and spending money."

"I think it's silly when they say there's a twenty percent chance of rain and its pouring outside," laughed Charvette unusually loud.

The day was slow, giving Alyx the time she needed to work on the projects that had fallen behind. A few regular customers had come in during the day to check for new merchandise and bring goodies for the cats, and we rewarded with loud purrs.

The threatening storm clouds swirling overhead all afternoon had gathered into a serious thunderstorm by early evening, releasing torrential rain with no sign of letting up. Charvette was with a customer when Rupert Moresby walked in and stood by the counter. Pooky let out a yowl and ran off somewhere, the reason unknown to anyone. Misty chased after her, and I took an Egyptian cat pose on the checkout counter. Charvette acknowledged Moresby's presence with a clandestine nod and he left. Then, she left for her dinner break as soon as she finished with her customer.

On Friday evenings, employees had two hours for dinner. They could go whenever they chose as long as they were back by eight o'clock. Both Alyx and Maggie felt very strongly about two people always being in the store for closing, not because there had been any trouble but only because they wanted to play it safe.

While she waited for Charvette to get back, Alyx kept busy looking for the perfect place to hang the latest item George had dropped off that morning—a child's chair turned into a shelf. The last customer had left half an hour earlier. Tired and bored, Alyx broke the store's rule of always having two people in the store at closing, locked the front door, and started to close out the cash register.

She had just put the cash in a zippered bag and was stepping out from behind the counter when the back door opened and shut with a thud. She called out a greeting to Charvette, proceeding towards the office to secure the money in the safe until she could get it ready for deposit.

Suddenly, there was a sharp crack of thunder from above followed by another sound, a loud pop. My natural instincts forced me to run for cover. A bullet whizzed by me and lodged in the back of the wing chair to Alyx's right. Confused as to the direction of the shot, she dropped behind the couch in front of her.

I heard another shot fired, this time striking the wall behind her. Rain was still coming down hard but the thunder was moving away.

"If its money you want, you can have it." She tossed the bag in the direction the last shot had come from. "You don't have to kill me. I don't know who you are or even what you look like. You have nothing to fear. Just take it and go."

Alyx crawled on her hands and knees to the end of the couch and peered around the corner. Charvette, dripping wet hair, mascara running down her cheeks, was holding the handgun kept in the desk drawer in the office. She spoke in a strange, hollow voice from a place beyond my understanding:

"Money, that's all everybody thinks about; you, Rupert, Novie. Well, guess what Alyx," she hissed waving the gun around, "I don't want your money."

Alyx froze in place. "Then, what do you want?"

"It's all your fault, you know. You ruined it all. He was going to divorce her and marry me," she said with a sob.

I took a position on top of a tall bookshelf, just to the right of Charvette.

Alyx kept her voice level as she looked around for something she could use to defend herself.

"I don't understand. What do I have to do with that?"

"Oh, you have plenty to do with it. It's your fault she changed her mind," Charvette kept babbling. "He was just waiting till she sold the building so he could get his business back up and running. You talked her out of it. She was going to sell until she heard you weren't. She told him you discussed your reasons for not selling and she was inspired to hold on to her dream. What about my dreams, Alyx? What about my dreams?" she whimpered.

"Charvette, you're wrong, I didn't talk her out of anything."

"Oh, yes, you did. I saw you and your stupid cat talking to her yesterday."

Charvette was becoming more agitated now, waving the gun around.

Alyx quickly crawled to the end of the couch, grabbed the paperweight she had spied earlier and threw it, missing her by a couple of feet.

In that instant, I lunged at Charvette from the top of the bookshelf, knocking the gun out of her hand and batting it out of the way when it hit the floor. She didn't see Pooky behind her heels, stepped back, lost her balance, and fell on her ample behind. Misty came out of the shadows and pounced on her, biting her everywhere, shredding her with her back feet while Charvette screamed, "Get them off of me!"

Alyx scrambled for the fallen weapon, picked it up, and leveled it at her until the police arrived.

Much later, Charvette told the police the whole story. She knew Rupert's business was failing and that he had approached Dunne Development with the luxury condominium idea, investing heavily without Novie's knowledge.

He promised Charvette he would divorce his wife and marry her when he received his share of the profit. James Dunne originally told Rupert the only way he could go forward with the project was to have at least one of the buildings next to one of his or it wouldn't be worth it. When it looked like Alyx and Maggie weren't going to sell, Rupert pressured his wife to sell. When he told Charvette that his wife had made her final decision after talking with Alyx, Charvette snapped. Some said that since she couldn't get mad at him, she turned her anger against Alyx.

The *Beachside Journal* ran a full story on the incident, including what the writer called our *heroic* actions. Some people were skeptical about the role we played, arguing that we only reacted on instinct, while others joked that we knew exactly what we were doing and had planned the whole thing. Alyx could only speculate. All I can say is that if I'd acted on instinct alone, I'd still be cowering under a piece of furniture, and that goes for Misty and Pooky as well.

On the same page of the newspaper, Alyx read an article about a purse-snatching ring. The article said the Beachside police had solved a tri-city string of robberies that involved purse snatching, the purses being returned within the hour with nothing missing. The thieves, mostly teen juvenile delinquents, stole the purse, had a duplicate made of the owner's house key and then looked for the purse owner's home address, usually found in the wallet.

They had cracked the case when they found two men who looked like they had encountered attack cats at the last home they tried to burglarize. The officer who found them said they had had plenty of time to get away before he arrived, but apparently they had been too traumatized to make a move. Beachside Police arrested the accused ringleader—Dan Ramsey, owner of Ramsey's Collectibles on Ocean Street—when they searched the store and found a notebook with a list of addresses that matched those of the homes burglarized.

"What greater gift than the love of a cat?"—Charles Dickens

CHAPTER FORTY-TWO: *The Dinner Party*

The following day, I heard Alyx cancel the dinner at the restaurant. She opted, instead, to host a dinner party at home to celebrate Ethan's release and all other good things that deserved a celebration.

"Murfy, you and your friends are invited too," she said as she hung up the phone.

The night of the dinner party, Alyx paid more than the usual attention to her appearance. She couldn't decide what to wear. She stood in front of her closet, pulling one outfit after another off the hangers, holding them up to her front, and then hanging them back up with disgust. The girls and I were getting dizzy watching her. Amazed at what she saw, Misty wondered if there was something wrong with Alyx. I said she was nervous about seeing that lawyer, David Hunter.

Misty and Pooky were all excited until Alyx decided on a generic black dress which, according to Misty was more suited for a funeral than a party. Alyx laid the dress out on the bed, undressed and stepped in the shower.

Misty immediately jumped on it, intent on destroying it, and invited Pooky and me to join her in the fun. I ran off, not wanting any part in what the girls were doing. Minutes later, I heard the water shut off and I sneaked back into the room. As I predicted, Alyx wasn't happy when she came out of the shower and saw the felines resting comfortably on her dress.

"Oh, no!" she moaned, "Look what you've done to my dress. Now what am I going to wear?"

Alyx sat on the bed and dialed a number.

"Maggie, I don't have anything to wear. I have thirty minutes to get ready for company, and I have nothing to wear. I had a dress picked out—that black sleeveless sheath I wear to all parties—laid it on the bed while I showered, and the cats got on it, bunched it all up and it's full of cat hair. Any suggestions?"

Alyx laughed. "Yes, you're right; the cats do have good taste, and yes, it is just a dinner and not a lifetime commitment. I'll see you shortly."

Maggie arrived and helped Alyx select a soft, flowered chiffon skirt, and a mauve, spaghetti strapped silk top, with a lacy, deep V-neckline. She wore no jewelry, but did wear sandals. Satisfied she didn't look too dressed up, Alyx joined Ethan in the living room to wait for the rest of the guests.

Ethan didn't bring a date. He told Alyx he wasn't ready to bring anyone home to meet the family. He had finally called Lea and told her what was in his heart. As it turned out, she hadn't lied to him after all. Her friend, Steve, had spent the night, but on the couch—he was just a friend as she had told Ethan. Ethan and Lea parted on a friendly note, recognizing they weren't right for each other anymore.

"Thanks for the party, Mom."

"I'm thankful we can do this. It could have just as easily gone the other way; I could be visiting you in jail or you could be visiting my grave."

"I don't ever want to go through that again if I can help it. The arrest alone was enough to traumatize me."

"You haven't told me what happened. Do you feel like talking about it?"

"I don't mind talking about it. Two thoughts wiggled through my head when Smarts said I was under arrest.

One consisted of what if they never find who did it? The other—I didn't do anything. The latter made me mouthy, making me look even guiltier.

"My feelings were certainly not spared when we arrived at the police station. They roughed me out of the car, the handcuffs bruising the bones under my skin. Once inside, I was pressed against a cold wall with eight others. After standing in line for over three hours, I was finally called to the window, where there was the meanest woman I've ever had the misfortune of speaking to.

"Everything was taken out of my pockets and placed into a plastic container, sealed with its own special number, in case I ever got out to claim it. From there, they placed me in a holding cell for a good five hours before I was given any food, or allowed to make phone calls. From the conversations going on around me, it seemed everyone was eager to share their story of how and why they were there. It was like a social gathering of misfits, and I didn't want any part of it. I patiently waited in the corner for one free phone call, thinking about whom to call. Maggie said she would have called a lawyer. I thought about calling Dad. In the end, I called no one."

"We survived this, Ethan, and we're the better for the experience." She took his arm, "Come on. I'll buy you a drink."

Alyx looked over the table setting, making sure nothing was missing, lit the candles, and greeted everyone as they came in. The dinner—shrimp scampi and rice catered by Angelo's on the River smelled delicious; the dessert, a bowl of fresh fruit and cannoli, not so much. She added croutons and cubed Feta cheese to the salad of mixed baby greens when her brother, Tom, arrived with his wife, Susan. Tom joined Ethan, who mixed him his drink of choice.

Maggie and George walked in with David Hunter. Alyx was talking to David when Bob arrived. Maggie, wearing a sleeveless, pale yellow, lightweight linen dress answered the door, looking uncomfortable in her role as greeter.

Alyx excused herself and went to her friend's rescue.

"Hi, Bob; I'm glad you could make it," and looking around him added, "Is Helen with you?"

"No, she couldn't make it; she's allergic to cats."

Maggie appeared to stifle a laugh when Alyx glared at her. To everyone's relief, Ethan approached his father and led him to where the bar was set up.

"Maggie, behave yourself. Give him a break," Alyx pleaded, "Do it for Ethan's sake."

"Okay, you're right; he has tried to redeem himself and who am I to hold a grudge if you and Ethan are willing to forgive him."

Ethan asked everyone to take a seat around the table and Alyx raised her wine glass for a toast.

"Thank you all for coming to my celebration of all good things and for your help and support during a difficult period in my life and Ethan's; I don't know what I would have done without you." She turned to Ethan, "Do you have anything you want to say?"

"What Mom said goes for me too. Thank you."

My roommates and I strutted to the kitchen for the shrimp and rice that Alyx had spooned into our bowls before she sat down to dinner, and we had our own celebration.

THE END

ABOUT THE AUTHOR

 Anna Kern didn't just have an imaginary friend—as a child, she had imaginary friends who stayed with her way past childhood. She made up stories in her head and dreamed of one day having a book published, but it wasn't until later in life that she wrote her first novel.

She recently retired from a public school system in Florida and moved to St. John's County to be closer to her son, James. She shares her condominium with her cats Pooky and Misty who keep her amused and amazed. Murfy lives with her son and visits often.

A Paw-sible Theory is her first cozy mystery.

www.ingramcontent.com/pod-product-compliance
Lightning Source LLC
Chambersburg PA
CBHW020328260626
47156CB00004B/1429